Finch Books by Lanne Garrett

Single Books
The Cinder City Embers: Singularity

A Cursed Crow
The Seven Year Crow
The Court of Less
The Song of Blood and Bones
A Court of One
A Curse So Dark and Twisted
A Reign of Ruin
Broken Wings and Wicked Things

A Cursed Crow

BROKEN WINGS AND WICKED THINGS

LANNE GARRETT

Broken Wings and Wicked Things
ISBN # 978-1-80250-776-8
©Copyright Lanne Garrett 2024
Cover Art by Erin Dameron-Hill ©Copyright May 2024
Interior text design by Claire Siemaszkiewicz
Finch Books

Published in 2024 by Finch Books, United Kingdom.

BROKEN WINGS AND WICKED THINGS

Dedication

To Ran, with all my heart.

You spotted snakes with double tongue,

Thorny hedgehogs, be not seen;

Newts and blind-worms, do no wrong;

Come not near our fairy queen.

— excerpt from *Fairy Land ii* by William Shakespeare.

Elphame

- Alfheim -
The Golden Court

Spring Court

Seelie Courts

Summer Court

The Court
of Blood
and Bones

Wildelands   The Gate

The Court of
Shadows

The Court of Less

Unseelie Courts

The
Hallows

- Tylwyth -
Winter Court

Autumn
Court

Chapter One

Hell can be found between two moments. Entire lifetimes are lived, destinies are decided, worlds are built and destroyed, life is given and taken just as quickly. Between these points, no matter how short or long they may be, the fates decide what the next will bring. Nothing stops fate or her cruel touch. And she walked today through the fields of Elphame, just as she had down the streets of Whitwick, looking for me. Like the last time she reminded me of her incredible power, I would crumple under her weight again. She walked slowly while I enjoyed little slivers of peace in a world made for war. She was like that, slapping her surprise across your face just as you got comfortable. Her claws would dig at my insides like choices not yet made — and regret for those yet to come. That's what happened when you ignored the inevitable. It needled you until you bled to death from the holes of ignorance.

It was not bliss — ignorance. It was a punishing and cruel death. It was suffering and looking back, seeing where it all went wrong and knowing you could have prevented it from happening had you acted sooner. It was foolish hope that the inevitable would spare you. Win or lose, there was nothing blissful about willful blindness.

There were few cast-iron certainties in Elphame. But one thing I knew for sure was that nothing lasted forever — not war and not peace, not life — and for some of us, not even death. Nevertheless, we still tried to hold on to the good bits for as long as we could. We each held a death grip on the moments that brought us a brief respite from the calamity that is Elphame, however fleeting they may be. It was worth the struggle to hold on. In those instances, between heaven and hell, we found reasons to get back up, to keep pushing forward, to look death in the eyes and hold on for dear life. We found the courage to stand on the frontlines, shoulder to shoulder with those we love, and motion for our enemies to take their best shot.

And that's what fate brought our way again — enemies to face and trials to overcome. It would not be Elphame if we weren't preparing for another war. We had not heard the last from the mortal world. With each passing day, we risked more to a realm we knew would make a final stand against us. Although I was born in Whitwick Gates, it was no longer my home. Where I'd once felt conflicted and tried to protect my people to my death, I was no longer torn between realms. I wouldn't risk my life for those who cared nothing for me, who treated me like I was just another one of the monsters. I'd tried to save them and had been chased away with the rest of the Fae. I would not willingly bleed for them again.

The oath between man and Fae was gone, thrown away by the mortals, and I feared the results would be devastating for us all. The cost would be felt across both realms, because no one escapes the price we pay. No one is free from the suffering of war, no matter which side of the field you stand on. Like fate, war was a bitch and spared no one the grief of his touch. The graves would be dug by us all. Some would die, and some would only wish for the sweet mercy of death. Memories had that way about them, when it was all said and done, to make you regret not dying with the others rather than live with what you did to survive. I was walking proof of that.

This time, though, we'd be prepared. We wouldn't leave it to chance or to fate. It would be a bloodbath if we waited on Whitwick to make their first move. If the mortal world stepped through the Gate, those who didn't wither away from Fae sickness would be slaughtered. There would be no more warnings. Whatever man decided to do, we'd be ready for it. Solas wasn't one to gamble, especially not where I was concerned. I had been the target too many times for him to sit idly by and wait on others to decide on war. He wanted plans over plans, because he didn't win every war by waiting for the other side to choose whether standing toe to toe with him was a risk worth taking. Swift and merciless decisions won wars, not hesitation or clemency.

Blood and Bones stood before me, and it took my breath away. It didn't matter how many times I had seen the wall surrounding the original court of Elphame. I was still taken aback by the clotted and macabre appearance of it. Centuries of spilled blood stained the walls, darkening over the years to something almost black and utterly revolting. As far as the eye could see, a dark obsidian wall flanked the border. The sight of it was enough of a warning to make all who came here rethink their life choices and turn around. It looked like it had been carved from a mountain, encircling the court from all sides. Not many had been inside the original court, and most who had attempted it under the rule of a dead woman, Solene, were what created the walkway into the once-upon-a-time hell of Elphame.

The first time I had stepped beyond the wall in search of answers, the dried blood had flaked off under my touch. I could hear the sound of it peeling away like a crusted leaf underfoot. It had made my skin crawl and my mind conjure images of my death. The memory of it had the same effect.

We walked up the crushed bone path, through the skeletons and long-rotted parts, to the notorious wall. The bones crunched under my boots, and it took everything I had not to vomit. Like the last time, the sound reminded me of my first day in Elphame and the pathway into the Golden Court. I'd never liked this place when I'd first come — but I liked it even less now. I had almost died when I had been in the basement of Blood and Bones, the day I'd come for a knife to kill the Caller of Crows. I had been stabbed, saved three Aos Si prisoners and waged a war I wasn't ready for. Here's hoping this visit wouldn't be like my last. I wasn't holding my breath, however. Nothing surprised me in Elphame.

For Solas and Zephyr, coming to Blood and Bones was like going home to their childhood. Neither looked bothered by the sights. Their boots crunched the bones to dust and fazed them none. But they *were* war and nightmares. Walking on the backs of the dead was not unusual for the two men who were the very reason people were afraid of the dark. Seeing them banter back and forth was unnerving. Their laughter rolling over the bone graveyard was an uncomfortable combination of horror and revelry. It was no different than hearing them laugh on the battlefield. They could ignore the bodies a lot longer than I could have. I was still too new to the world of war. It still bothered me to see it. For me, coming to Blood and Bones was nothing more than memories I didn't want, of being desperate enough to kill. And each step I took brought fresh emotions of my last trip into the basement of this awful place. But that was what it meant to lead, to win, to protect those weaker. We tainted our souls. We faced our horrors and gave ourselves new nightmares. We were always ready to look into the dark corners of the world, stepping over those in our way and planning the exits before our enemies swallowed us whole.

Within the breeze that swirled the bone dust into little funnels, I could almost hear Seth's wings in the background, the Gargoyle's last flight. Seth had died the last time I had come to Blood and Bones. He'd given his life for me to end the Taking of the Crows. The tingling in my thigh grew, and I glanced back once, hoping I'd see the Gargoyles, but they had been gone since the day we'd killed Solas' sister, Solene. The Gargoyles had taken Seth's stone body home, wherever that was. It was their custom to place his rocky statue at the gates to their home as a reminder of who died to protect their realm. Every now and again, when my nightmares became too much, I could feel a faint draft from wings I couldn't see and knew it was him. There had been so many deaths since my arrival in Elphame, but his was one of my greatest regrets. I had been told he'd died a glorious death, but he hadn't. There was no beauty to be found when a life as great as his was taken. War is ugly. Death is hideous. Everything else is a lie we tell when it hurts too bad to be honest with ourselves.

"Your little pet is following us." Nix stood on my shoulder, looking behind us. His feet danced side to side as I navigated a path I didn't want to fall on. The day Seth had died, I had skinned my hands and knees as I was thrown onto the ground. I'd needed to pick shards of bones from my skin for days. The thought of doing it again made my stomach flop and reminded me to be careful of my footing.

"I know. My thigh is tingling. Every time the Sluagh are near, my scar acts up," I replied. I looked back and watched a small Sluagh making his way over the bone path toward me. "Why is he following me?"

"Because you claimed him," Solas answered from a few yards ahead of us, his ear always tuned to my voice. "He hasn't left since you leashed him. The other day, I found him in the library in front of the fireplace."

"I let him in. It was raining," I replied.

"He's not your pet," Solas called back to me.

"I told him to stay at home." I flushed. I turned to the creature and motioned for him to pick up his pace. "If you're coming, hurry up. I don't like standing around out here. It makes my skin crawl."

"So eager to be bitten again?" Solas asked and laughed. "Your landing will be worse on these rocks than at home on the grass."

I winced at the memory and held my ribs. I chanced a look around, and although I couldn't see the other Sluagh, they'd be wherever Solas was. I could feel them watching me from the shadows of the forest. Their eyes felt like prickly needles along my spine. The small one made his way to me and walked at my side in an awkward shuffle and drag. He walked on his two back legs and used the crook of his wings as his hands. He looked like a bat trying to walk instead of fly. It was both awkward to watch and terrifying to see.

Somehow, he looked scarier without the grace found in the sky.

"What's your name?" I asked, patting the top of his head. His head came up to my ribcage. "I can't just call you 'the smaller Sluagh'."

"Sluagh do not speak, Perdi," Solas called back and shook his head.

"How do they communicate if they can't speak?" I asked.

"They follow Solas and communicate in their own ways," Nix replied. "They aren't of Elphame, so the rest of us don't understand them."

"I shall call you...Milo," I finally said and smiled. "Yes, that's a good name."

"If he were a mortal dog, which he's not," Solas called out. "Again, he's not your pet."

"But he's still mine," I answered.

"Up until you lose your hand," Solas countered. "And so that you're aware, you can't regrow limbs if a Sluagh decides to bite them off. Their wounds can't be fixed by Elphame magick. Just look at your thigh. Don't say I didn't warn you."

I leaned in closer to Milo. His spicy scent filled my chest and calmed me in ways only monsters could. "You're mine."

He looked up, and for a moment I swore he understood me. Or, he was hungry and was sizing me up for how much he could get down before they made him spit me out. I was willing to bet on the latter.

"If you're going to eat me, make it quick," I whispered to him. "But trust me when I tell you, hell spit me back out. No one likes the taste of Crow once they've had a bite. I'm too bitter to swallow."

Nix muttered from my shoulder that he wouldn't climb into Milo's mouth to rescue me, should I be eaten for my stupidity. I ignored his warnings, as I often did. We followed Solas and Zephyr through the wall, and I froze. I didn't like being there. I didn't like how it felt against my skin or soul and hated the smell even more. The heat pressed against me, and the sweat that had started before I had even stepped into the wall now trickled down my spine, leaving a cold trail on my skin. Milo chittered from behind me and nudged my back, forcing me forward with his head. I wanted to scold him. I didn't like to be rushed toward doom any quicker than the next sane person, but I swallowed my anger. Milo chittered again, and I stopped in my tracks.

Small rocks fell from above, and I told myself not to look to see what I could hear scratching at the stone wall. Whatever haunted the walls of Blood and Bones wasn't something I needed to view today. Milo looked up, his chittering finally stopping. I followed his stare and froze. Holding on to the walls were small and colorful winged creatures, some no bigger than a potato. For a moment, I thought they were Sluagh and relaxed. But once their wings shimmered, changing their colors, I knew they weren't. They reminded me of fairytale dragons told to children as bedtime stories. A bright orange one snapped his teeth in the air, and I flinched at the sound of whatever it had eaten. They may have been no bigger than two feet long, on the larger end, but I wasn't foolish enough to think that size mattered in any way, not in Elphame. Slowly, dozens of them began their climb down the wall, and a small scream escaped my lips.

"What the fuck are those?" I squeezed out. My words were barely audible.

"Dragons," Nix answered as if that would be enough. "Don't worry. They eat bugs and grubs and fruit. They're harmless and pretty friendly, if you give them a chance."

"Where the hell did they come from?" I asked. "I've never seen one before."

"They've always been in Elphame. Many creatures are coming out of hiding now that Solene is dead. She used to kill the smaller Fae for no other reason than being able to do it. Many of the smaller, defenseless Fae hid from her sight," Nix replied. "Now that Blood and Bones is a refuge, the dragons have returned."

"Because the place isn't scary enough?" I muttered.

"Most would say the Court of Shadows is worse," he said with a laugh. "And you don't have a problem strolling around in there."

"I don't stroll through the Court of Shadows. I run," I answered. "I'm not that stupid."

Nix cleared his throat. "This coming from the Crow with a pet Sluagh?"

"Point made," I replied.

Nix moved to my other shoulder and reached his hand to one of the dragons. Before I could pull back, the dragon scurried toward Nix's hand for attention. I waited for it to latch onto a few digits but heard a soft purr as Nix scratched the tiny beast's head.

"Not everything here is meant for war, Perdi," Nix said. "You see the worst in all creatures because it's all you've been shown since coming here. If you stop long enough, you'll find that most of us want to live in peace and are only forced to become monsters. Many of us haven't had the chance to live as we'd like." Nix patted the dragon and left them be. "If you're lucky enough to bond with a thunder of dragons, you'll have friends for life. They're more likely to be found in gardens, eating insects, rather than fighting for territory or titles. I'd give my arm to have a few of these guys protecting our gardens from pesky slugs or beetles. Plus, it would irritate Zephyr and Solas to see we had invited dragons to live in the backyard. Solas is already attacked daily by the pixie clan. Could you imagine dragons going after him every time he stepped into the backyard?"

"The stories we were told as children said dragons breathed fire," I replied. "I'm starting to wonder if our fables were based on the creatures of Elphame more than our imaginations."

"Oh yeah, these little guys can roast a marshmallow or two," Nix replied. "Or singe a few of Solas' hairs." Nix pointed at the wall. "When we first walked in, their colors were vibrant and rotating, in a warning to the others. Now, they're calm and no longer shifting. And all it took was a moment of kindness. Sometimes, that's all we ever need, a break from what Elphame throws our way. One act of kindness can mean the difference between life and death."

I laughed at the imagery of Solas putting out small fires in the backyard. The break we had taken, to look beyond first impressions, to see life over death, was enough to settle the urge to run. Blood and Bones wasn't my favorite place, but our shared moment was a good start at building new memories. In all his war talk and willingness to eat his way through a battlefield, Nix tried first for compassion and understanding. It was something I was trying to relearn since coming to Elphame—how to be more than the nightmare Elphame had forced me to become.

"Thank you, Nix, for always making sure I see things through the eyes of love rather than war."

"Elphame is scary enough. We shouldn't create fear where it ought not be," he replied. "I'm getting myself a dragon. If you can have a Sluagh, I can have a dragon."

"It's only fair," I answered and laughed.

"You're not here alone, Perdi. We're all in this together," Nix replied. "It's not as scary when you remember that you're not alone."

I inched my way through the halls of Blood and Bones, with a small beast pushing me from behind, eventually guiding me into a large room where a massive stone table sat with chairs. I scanned the room for an alternate exit and found none. If all hell broke loose, there was only one way in or out. I didn't like those odds. I hated being in a room with one door. How Zephyr was so calm was beyond me. He either knew of a different way out of the room or knew he could kill them all and not need any other escape plan.

"They'll never be able to hold you," Nix whispered from my shoulder. "Don't worry. I've got your back. On my own, I can buy you enough time to get out of here."

I smiled. Nix was a good gnome to have on my side. I'd seen firsthand what gnomes could do to an army of warriors. Standing between a gnome and their family was suicide.

"Thanks, Nix."

Chapter Two

With still rattled nerves, I took a seat between Solas and Zephyr. Nix jumped onto the table, and Milo sat against the wall behind me. Lily, a Seer, was the only other face that I recognized. She looked at Milo, then shook her head. The expression on her face said that she, like Solas, thought I was gambling with my life by bonding with a Sluagh. They may have been right but getting to where I stood had been a chance everyone else had bet against. And yet, here I was, still alive. Although, in fairness, I *had* died once and have come close on a few more occasions since then. Of all the choices I've made to date, standing this close to the Sluagh was not the worst one I've made.

The room we were in was familiar. It was the last room I had been in when I came for Solene. Finn had been the first one sent in. He had grabbed Solene before she could wield her magick. I still remember the look on his face. Although he was cocky, as usual, he looked like he was in pain, like holding on to Solene had been a fate worse than death. And after peeling away her mind like an onion, I wouldn't have wanted to put my hands on her either. Her soul was an ugly thing to touch.

"Perdi?" Lily's voice called me out of my head.

"Sorry. I blanked out," I replied and felt my face grow warm. "I haven't ever come here without war chomping on my heels. It's unnerving. I keep waiting for something bad to happen."

"It's okay. This place *is* unnerving, and war is never satiated in Elphame. Unfortunately, I can't get the blood off these walls, and there will always be a reason for war. But know you are always safe within our borders." She smiled in understanding. "I was just telling the others about the Gate and what we felt when the magick began to change within it. Are you able to comment on it? Your experience may be a little different than ours."

I nodded and thought back to the day Finn and I had stepped into the Gate. "The Gate itself hasn't really changed. There's just more of it, like something else has been added. Whatever was added shouldn't be there and was placed by someone else. It's new and unstable, and anger isn't a good enough word to describe how it feels. If you could see revenge, that is what it would look like — tinted black and starved of life. When Finn and I stepped inside, it still felt like the Gate, only the air held hate, rage and vengeance. It is like every single emotion mortals have toward Fae is bottled up in there." I sucked in a shaking breath. The memory of the Gate made me sink deeper into my seat, as if the very recalling of the information could somehow hurt me. "Finn had said that the Gate felt like waiting on decisions to be made, on whether we're going to war or not. He said the only place he had felt that much rage and terror was on the battlefield with bodies at his feet.

He, like me, felt it all directed at Elphame. He said it was directed at me."

Lily's face told me she had felt the same thing as we had. "Has anything changed since that day?"

"Since I'm not linked to it as I once was, I don't feel any changes, unless I'm using the Gate or standing inside it," I answered and thought about it for a moment. "I haven't felt anything usual or off, aside from what I originally felt the day Finn and I were in there. But I stay away from it, like everyone else does. We just walked by it, and I didn't feel anything that made me need to stop to check it out. I can say that it's not like the last time I got too close to it, when I felt that burst of power and a forceful pull. Whatever it was that tried to drag me toward it wasn't there an hour ago."

"When did you stop feeling the Gate?" she asked.

"When there wasn't a Darkmore spell on the Gate left for me to feel," I replied. "I was never attached to anything other than the actual spells on the Gate. The tear or rift between realms? I can't feel that unless I step into it. What we call 'the Gate' — or the place between now and then — was never tied to me any more than it was linked to you or your neighbor."

"What do you mean, 'now and then'?" one of Lily's people asked.

"When you step beyond the wall into the place where the Gate once was, it is a place of here and there, now and then, a place linked in time but apart from either realm. Time isn't the same there. It's everything at once and nothing at all. Before, when Darkmore blood held the Gate, I could see the past. I've seen Aoife in there and watched when she first walked through that Gate, along with countless others," I answered. "But when Solene met her fate, I stopped seeing the Crows of the past."

"And now?" Lily asked.

"Now, when I step through the Gate, I can see Elphame on one side and Whitwick on the other. Sometimes they look as they are. Other times they look as they once were. I don't know if what I see is magick or if it's memories or emotions trapped. Perhaps it's being a Darkmore witch that has allowed me to see what I've seen…or maybe it's being a Finis that allows me to hear and feel souls. I'm not sure." I replied and couldn't think of a better way to describe something that was everything and nothing at once. It was impossible to explain unless they could see what I saw. "Whatever magick or energy holding the Gate open has created a bubble frozen in time. It feels like all the years gone are being held in a hitched breath, along with the emotion of all who have passed through it. Every time I step through, I'm waiting for that breath to release, like waiting for a decision to finally be made. At least, that's what it's like for me."

Lily nodded. "I get the same impression when I've crossed. The energy of the Gate is familiar magick, only I can't place it."

"It feels like Elphame, only more of it," I replied. "In some ways, the energy in the Gate is purer, stronger than out here. It's raw, pure, unfiltered and unshared. There's so much power in there that you can't breathe. It cramps your muscles if you stay too long. It's hard to move around without feeling weighed down by it. It prickles along your skin, and to take from it is death. The payment for interfering with it was my life."

"Did we come here to trade theories about the Gate? That could have been done over a meal at the manor," Zephyr asked and leaned forward. His hands were clasped on the table, polite, unlike his tone. "Lily, you've called us here for a reason, and this time you asked for Perdi to come. Let's cut to the chase. You don't idly ask for anything."

"No, I don't," she replied and turned her attention back to me. "Perdi, would you be willing to check on the Gate again to see what is happening?"

Zephyr tensed beside me. "I do not feel comfortable with that."

"Nor do I," Solas added.

"Unless you both now go by the name of Perdi, I didn't ask either of you." She brushed them off with a wave of her hand. She didn't fear them as much as everyone else did. But she, like me, had no problem looking into the eyes of terror and laughing. Her focus landed back on me, and I fought against the urge to squirm. "How do *you* feel about that, Perdi? Forget about the expectations of all others. Their fears and wants mean nothing when you are the one who must live with your decisions and suffer your consequences."

"At one time, I'd do it. Now, I don't want to," I replied. I was brave but not stupid and brave at once. My curiosity didn't stretch that far anymore. "I don't know what's going on with the Gate or what's caused that new magick, and I don't care enough to be the sacrificial lamb. You'll need to find some other way. I will help as much as possible, but I'm not stepping foot into that Gate. I don't want to die."

Lily smiled. "Well, there's a first time for everything."

Zephyr relaxed beside me. "We need a different plan, one that doesn't involve Perdi sticking her neck out for it."

Solas sighed. "I'd sooner not risk her life, but Perdi will do as her soul commands."

"We see war." Lily finally dropped the other shoe I had been waiting for.

"Fucking Seers," Zephyr grumbled.

Lily didn't take it as an insult and smiled. Seers rarely had anything good to say when they were the ones to start the conversation. And their news was usually the same every time—war, death, pain, suffering. "We see a great battle coming but cannot see who is fighting. We also do not know when it will arrive. We see mortals, but not where they fit into the puzzle or what land they will stand on. We can feel pain, horror, sadness and utter despair. There will be many deaths, both Fae and mortal. The cost of winning will attract the notice of the Gods and Goddesses. A great payment will be made to end the war—and an even greater cost for how it ends. We do not see who will pay, but we all will feel it, just the same."

"Which means it'll involve one of us in this room...or all of us," Solas answered.

"Accurate enough," Lily replied. "While I don't see Perdi in the middle of it, specifically, I can feel it. And since I can't see her, I know the Gate plays a part. We've never seen the fates of those on the other side of the Gate. Mortals are tied to Perdi."

I groaned. "I hate that cursed Gate."

"As do most of us, Perdi," Lily answered. "The Gate is still off limits to all, but I believe we should move as many as possible out of the Court of Less and maintain a close watch for now. Whatever is going to happen, the Gate will be the reason. It is central to everything we've seen so far. It will be the cause of a bloodbath, and we all will bleed for it. We all will feel the fallout of this war for years to come."

"We need to prepare for whatever the mortals are planning to do," Lily said.

I began to fidget as they spoke about war. It wasn't just any war, though. It was war against mortals. I moved from the table and grabbed some food once they began talking about battles that I knew nothing about, in a time when Whitwick was nothing more than a Gate and a few holes in the ground. Nix paced the table and shot down many of their ideas. He knew mortals better than the rest of them. He had spent a decade with me in Whitwick and knew what it was like during a Taking. He understood the reasons behind their rage and their need for retribution. More than that, his people were known to conquer in a matter of minutes and leave such horror in their wake that no other man was brave enough to try for another round. Nix and Solas were of the same mind—how they could win without exerting more energy or manpower than needed. It was painful to listen to. My heart couldn't shift into war as quickly as the others could. I still saw mortals as people and couldn't see them as enemies without a face or name. While they planned for death, I wanted to save as many souls as I could, regardless of which side of the Gate they stood. But my bleeding heart was why it was always bruised and battered. My need to save the weaker was the reason I left pieces of my soul scattered from one end of Elphame to the other.

I sat along the edge of the room, where I was most comfortable, with Milo. While the others talked about a coming war, I found a small piece of happiness at the edge of a conversation that prickled against my soul. I watched Milo eat a small pile of fruits and an entire chicken, bone and all before he stopped pressing his nose against my hand for more. Milo huffed as he glanced above us. Two small dragons were inching down the wall toward my bowl of fruit. My first instinct was to wave them off. Instead, I picked up a grape and held it out. They were cautious at first, untrusting of how friendly I really was. I knew that feeling all too well. Those who showed you kindness either wanted something from you or were about to trap and torture you. I understood their hesitancy. Trust wasn't something easily given in Elphame. Instead of forcing them to choose between their safety and food, I rolled a couple of grapes a few feet away and watched as they collected them and scurried back up the wall. I tossed a few more berries into the corner for them. It costs nothing to show acts of kindness, to show mercy where you could and to hold on to your humanity for as long as possible. I wondered how long I'd have that opinion, how long it would take for me to understand that kindness, even my own, wasn't free.

I turned my focus back to the room and cringed when I picked up words of invasions and death. There was little room for mercy within these walls. But that was war. This was the cost of winning, shaving off as much of your humanity as you could without turning into a monster who needed to be hunted down and killed.

"Does any of this make sense to you?" I whispered to Milo. He stared at me but said nothing. "Yeah, that's pretty much all I have to add, as well."

Milo moved closer, and I leaned into his warmth and scent of hot leather and spice. The heat from his body relaxed my tension, and I finally closed my eyes, dozing off to the sounds from the table and their plans for combat against the mortal realm. The steady vibration of Milo's breathing drew my mind away from war and into the gentle pull of sleep. Bits and pieces of memory filled me, memories of Whitwick Gates that had scabbed long ago. They were both cherished and painful to remember, the parts of life I craved to get back to and accepted I'd never have again — the smell of grass and forest, untouched by Elphame magick, the way the wind lifted my hair and blew it around my head like flames while I ran through fields that had never seen a splash of blood or fallen soldier, the feel of rain or snow or crisp river water during a swim. It was the small things in life that we didn't think about until they were no longer there that were the hardest to let go of.

The memories twisted with darkness and were replaced with me walking through hundreds of dead bodies, their shadows being dragged behind me. I could feel the rage burning in my gut as I unleashed all of it upon those who couldn't run away fast enough. Held within that rage was pure vengeance and the most honest touch of hate I had ever felt before. I breathed in the stench of death and felt utter satisfaction. Fog curled around my legs, and I didn't recoil from it. Screams filled my ears, and I jerked from my dream to Solas kneeling in front of me. Lily had her hand on his shoulder, holding him back, while the Sluagh wrapped tighter around me. Milo growled from deep within, charging the room with static and warning. His body vibrated. Heat rolled off him in waves. Above my head, a few dozen dragons hissed at the others, small puffs of smoke billowing from their mouths.

"What?" I asked. "Did I miss something?"

"You were screaming, Perdi. I couldn't wake you up," Solas answered. "Your little pet tried to bite me."

"Milo, let me go." I patted his claws. "It's okay."

"No, little Crow, it is not. It won't ever be."

I tilted my head. "Did anyone else hear that?"

"No, I've heard nothing." Lily was the first to answer.

"Did you hear Milo?" I asked Solas.

"Who is…the Sluagh? You really named him Milo?" Solas asked, and I nodded. "No, I didn't hear him. They don't speak out loud. If he has spoken, no one else heard it."

"How did I hear him but you didn't?" I asked.

Solas kissed my temple and shrugged. "You shouldn't be able to hear them. That's the point I'm trying to make. You're not Sluagh or a Royal of the Dark Courts."

"But she is Finis," Lily answered. "Perdi, you hear souls — not words, but close enough. The Sluagh are not of Elphame magick, and they, like you, are a will of their own."

I nodded as if I understood her. I didn't. I rarely understood their riddles. But a lot of answers were like that with the Fae — simple and difficult, at once. Like asking why there are raindrops and being told it was because the snow falls.

I glanced up again. "What's up with the dragons? Give them a couple grapes, and this is the thanks I get?"

Lily snickered. "They came to Milo's call to help you and tried to fend off Solas. A couple of grapes, and you have built your own tiny army of butterflies."

"I'll take any army I can get. I'm not foolish enough to think their size means anything more than ease of hiding from others," I replied.

"True enough," Lily said and glanced at Nix, who was sitting in the middle of the table, arguing with the other Seers. "The gnomes are the only army the Seers fear. The wee folk are as fierce as any other army in Elphame, but the gnomes are downright terrifying."

"You make friends everywhere you go." Solas smiled. "When you started screaming, and I approached, Milo growled in a warning. When I didn't listen, his chittering called the dragons into the room. Dragons and the Sluagh have a long history together. The dragons first appeared in the caves of the Sluagh. During Solene's reign, they returned to the Court of Shadows for protection. Solene used to kill them, thinking they were carrying information between courts. They weren't. They're neutral for the most part but protective over their chosen people. We usually see the dragons with the younger Sluagh. It appears that Milo comes with a horde of his own."

"Nix is going to bring one home," I replied.

"There are worse things to invite into our home," Solas answered. "Having a thunder of dragons take up residence is a sign of good luck."

"I could use some of that luck," I replied.

I stood with the help of Solas. Zephyr leaned against the table, one eyebrow cocked, but he said nothing. He would have the answers to my question about Milo, but he would never give them to me in front of so many people. Zephyr hogged his secrets like a nymph and her trinkets. On the table behind Zephyr was a map of Whitwick, right down to the garbage cans and flower beds. I turned away, wincing at the reality. Solas and I would be formally oathing ourselves this year, and I'd be planning a wedding while preparing for war. It was not how I wanted to spend this year — or any year, for that matter. I understood why queens organized parties and left the rest for someone else to deal with. The pain of it all was too much. How do I plan for a future while the others prepare for death? I told myself this was what it took to survive, but my heart didn't believe it. Winning at all costs wasn't winning. It was conquering. It was nothing more than a well-planned funeral. How many souls could I really take before I begged someone to dig a grave with my name on it?

I pulled away from Solas. "I can't do this. This isn't me, Solas. I'm not this person. I thought I wanted to be ready, but I don't want to know when everyone will die and that it'll be by my hand or my decision. Worse, I don't want to be responsible for their deaths because I wasn't willing to decide. I'm sorry, but I can't help...not like this. I'm not this strong. This hurts too much, and I can't do it."

"It's okay. Never apologize for your heart and soul." He turned my hand over and kissed my palm. When his eyes met mine, I saw war reflecting back, and I wanted to look away. "You don't have to come here for these reasons. We can go back to talking about it at home, safe and away from the war table. It doesn't have to be this way."

"I'll see you at home." I kept pulling against his grip until he let go. "I can't stay in here." A wave of nausea rolled over me, and I started to sweat. My mouth watered under the burn of stomach bile. My stomach began to cramp. "I can't breathe. It's too hot in here."

"I love you." He kissed my forehead. "It'll be okay. We don't need to skin ourselves alive to do this. We'll find a way for you to know and have a voice in the matter, without you having to suffer for the knowledge."

"I love you, too," I whispered back. "See you at dinner?"

"Hell or high water, you know I'll be there," he replied.

The world could fall around us, and we'd still be home for dinner. At our table, we weren't royal, we weren't war, we weren't thrones and crowns. We were family. And in Elphame, a safe space to call home was everything. I didn't say good night to the others. I simply walked from the room. I had to get out of there, away from the determination to conquer at all costs. I needed air that didn't taste of dark energy, the kind that rolled off them as they spoke of death.

I followed the light breeze from the stuffy room to the wide-open sky. I craved the coolness held on the other side of the walls. Its promise to wash away the heated thoughts that curled in my mind drove my feet faster. With Milo on my heels, and dragons following along on the wall, I navigated the caverns. I flinched each time my arms touched the walls. I turned sideways in a sad attempt at convincing myself that I wasn't touching centuries of dried gore. The walls, wide enough to move freely, felt like they were closing in on me, crushing the air from my lungs. I hated small spaces. I burst from Blood and Bones, gasping lungfuls of fresh air.

"Little Crow." Finn, dressed in Aos Si black leathers, stood at the entrance to Blood and Bones. He had become one of my closest friends since the war I'd waged on Satyr Island and one of the very few who was trusted to protect me. He was never too far from me. "You smell of tears not yet shed."

"Home," I choked out. My stomach clenched, knotted and tight. I was clammy from the sweat and heat. It overwhelmed my body. My chest felt like someone was squeezing me. "Just...please, take me home."

"Perdi!" Solas called from the tunnels.

"Wicked position to be in, between a Finis and a fucking nightmare," Finn answered and tilted his head as if listening. "Bells?"

Finn grabbed my arms as the first jerk slammed into my body. My feet slid along the ground as I was pulled by a hand I couldn't see. I froze and closed my eyes, listening to a familiar sound echo through Elphame. I could hear the same bells Finn heard. My stomach cramped tighter. The tainted magick I had felt weeks ago, held within the Gate, coated my arms like little ants crawling over my flesh. Rage, terror, and hate covered me in a sweat, not of my own. It wormed its way into my gut and grabbed hold.

"The bells toll over Elphame. The Gate has opened," I whispered and held onto Finn. "Don't let me go! Don't let them take me!"

"Perdi!" Solas screamed my name. I could hear his panic and the pounding of his feet eating up the space between us. His voice echoed down the corridors, bouncing off the bloodstained walls. But he'd never get to me in time.

"Solas!" I reached for him as my body jerked away from Finn's hands.

I was in the air, being pulled backward. I screamed out to Solas, to Zephyr, to anyone who could save me. From the wall of Blood and Bones, the shadows exploded from every crack in the stone and darkened the sky as they soared through the air toward me. The shadows wrapped around me, but nothing they did could release me from the invisible grasp around my very soul. Milo was in the air and dove for me, but not even he could pull me from the sky. He tugged on my legs and clawed at my skin until I bled, and my joints threatened to pop from their sockets. Although it hurt like hell to be pulled in two directions, I clung to his feet and screamed for him not to let me go. Milo's screech carried over the wind, piercing my eardrums. In the distance, his people answered his call and filled the clouds with terror. Dragons from every corner of Elphame took to the air and zipped toward me like a twister of black leaves. They grabbed at my clothes and hair, but it was futile. I tried, in vain, to tug away the insidious tendrils holding me. I was torn between pulling the power from me and holding on to Milo. Fear gripped me, and I screamed.

"Perdi, we can't pull you away." The shadows twisted and turned, only to fail at their attempts to save me. "We're sorry."

"Solas!" I turned to see the Court of Less behind me and the shimmering wall waiting.

"We won't leave you." The shadows wrapped around me.

The wind was knocked out of me when I hit the ground, and the shadows crawled down my throat when I tried to scream again. My head bounced against the earth and rocks until I saw nothing but darkness and Finn running toward me. His fingertips gripped mine, and the world was eaten away. No fight was left in me, and I wondered if being awake and aware of my demise was better…or worse.

Chapter Three

This would be the day of my Taking. A sudden replay of that fateful day bombarded me. I had dreamed about it over and over and recalled vividly every moment like a book I had favored. Regrettably, there wasn't a minute I didn't remember. Revisiting your past had this way of reminding you of the moments you had almost forgotten, forgave or put to rest. It distorted memories, forming them into something you'd never part with, the scars too deep to let go of, the terror too great not to be haunted.

In my replay, it was almost time to leave Whitwick and the life I thought I'd have. I had seen my fate tick away like a clock in the eyes of Mary Jane Hilliard, who had sold me the last sweets I'd eat in the mortal world. After today, I'd hate the taste and smell, and I'd never want another sugary treat again. As I walked home, I watched the Pryor twins jump from the roof of their house, smiling. The sickening sound of their bones meeting the brick drive echoed in my ears. It would not be the last time I heard the smack of death or the grinding of bones. Death was far too common around here to escape the sound of it.

The fog was creeping into Whitwick, bringing with it the horrors of Fae and their promise of death. I should have been terrified. The day I was Taken, surely, I had been more afraid than I now was. I remembered being scared but couldn't think of a reason to be now. I knew I'd be the one to leave Whitwick. I would be the Crow of their choosing. There wasn't much to be afraid of once you knew you would be Taken and accepted the cards you were dealt. Those who couldn't come to terms with it had always suffered more. They had been the reason the Fae remained for so long.

Whitwick Gates, the only home I had known, looked as it always had. It was rough around the edges, pleasant in the middle, and devastatingly tragic once you got to the warm center. The truth of who the Fae were and what they did when they came could never be fully covered up in the mortal world, only hidden from the first glance. When Elphame spat its terrors onto mortal soil, little by little, the morality of Whitwick would rot away, leaving only the meaty bits of horror. And after every Taking, my soul cried from the tragedies we buried, the fear we ran from, the hideousness I knew would be coming again and again. The Fae always did and always would.

The little hairs on the back of my neck told me nothing would ever be the same again, not for anyone but especially not for me. Today would change my life. I glanced to my left. Faolan stood and silently watched me. And for the briefest moment, I thought he was someone I could trust, and I prepared to follow his every word. But I knew better. I knew who he really was. The façade of who he tried to be fell away. I now knew why he had come, but at the time, I loved him enough to trust a Fae. I was a foolish little Crow, even then. I tilted my head and watched his face. He wasn't surprised. He wasn't afraid. He knew, as I did, that although it was time to run, it wouldn't help. We both understood what would play out. He would offer me up to save his people. But even knowing I'd do the same as he had, I would have given myself to protect the innocent. It still hurt as much as the first time I found out. Being the sacrifice is what my people were to Elphame, but it cut so much deeper when you knew those you love were the ones who handed you over. Paying tithe once was bad enough.

Faolan pointed at my house, and I shook my head.

"Run." Faolan's words pushed at my shoulders.

The bells finally chimed, echoing their warning over Whitwick. But I hadn't needed to hear them to know what they meant and what followed when the first chime was heard. The Gates to Elphame had opened, and the fog had begun to spread like a disease. This time, I didn't run. I knew I was leaving with the Fae. There was no point in trying to hide. I had never seen what happened when they came. I had only ever glimpsed them from my front window. But this time, I would watch. I had nothing to lose anymore. I walked down the sidewalk as Fae entered the mortal realm.

Through the darkness, I watched creatures crawling and twitching as they passed. Fae, who lit up the night like the fires from hell, slinked by. Creatures grabbed on to those who had tried to make it home and dragged them off the streets, screaming. I froze and watched as mortals bargained with Fae for their safety and the protection of their children in exchange for entertainment only the Fae would enjoy. The screams in the background pushed against me, twisting me around in the dark like invisible hands. There would be no safety to be found in Whitwick today.

"Perdi…" Solas' voice carried over the wind, and I flinched.

Hearing my name made my stomach flop. Through the fog, over the terror and laughter, my name slithered through the darkness. The smell of sugar and sweets reminded me why no adults ate the stuff anymore. The bells mixed with the carnage, and they wouldn't stop until the Fae got their Crow. And they always got their Crow, no matter how many of us died beforehand. I followed Solas' voice back to my house. He stood on my front walk, watching my house. He rotated his shoulders, readying himself for the Taking. He was the man I had hated, the man who had dragged me from my home. The man I was about to marry was the very one who'd called my name from the darkness, taunting me, tempting me to give my life and freedom for the safety of Whitwick. If I came out willingly, it would end. But I knew I wouldn't go outside. None of us ever did. All the bravado we had convinced ourselves of, before our name was called, washed away, and we hid like everyone else.

I stepped into my house and watched from the front window. Nix crawled from under the couch. He talked in the background of royal Fae, who I knew would be coming. I watched as Solas toyed with the kids who ran by. Some would make it to see another day, while others he left in the streets in a tangled mess. They would be buried tomorrow if they could find all the pieces. Faolan appeared beside me, telling me that something felt off. I turned to him and remembered every word he had said that day in my living room. I had replayed it over and over those first few months at the Golden Court.

"How many people die at Fae hands during a Taking?" I asked him.

"The Fae do this to humans, you know this. When too many of us powerful gather together, it makes you all a little crazy. It's what we do for fun," Faolan answered as he had said before.

"That's not what I asked. How many people are dying at the hands of Fae?"

Faolan shrugged a very human shrug. "The Fae don't care for mortals, Perdi. I'm sorry, but it's true."

"You're not hunting a Crow. You're simply killing my people," I replied.

"Perdi..." A taunting voice stood just inches on the other side of our front door. "Perdita Darkmore. Open the door, little Crow."

The world tilted, and I was lying in the boat. My body shook with pain and sickness from walking through the Gate. Moments I didn't remember, blocked out by the pain of coming through the Gate when I was in and out of consciousness, stood out in perfect clarity. Solas cleaned his bloody hands off the side of the boat, with Nix yelling at him for fulfilling the nightmare he was.

"What do you expect from me, Nix?" Solas asked.

"For you to be the king you claim to be," Nix answered. "Year after year, you go into the mortal world and bleed it dry. And now you take Perdi? You didn't even tell me. I didn't even get to warn her."

"I think it went well. Crows usually don't even make it this far," Solas replied and took a seat.

Nix held my hair out of my vomit as I was sick. "I don't think she's going to make it. Help her."

"If she doesn't make it, she wasn't the one." Solas moved to the head of the boat.

"Hold on, Perdi." Nix ran his hand down the back of my head. "Please, don't give up. Someone, please, help me."

Little creatures crawled out from behind crates and under seats and helped Nix keep me alive. Small bursts of energy helped soothe the burning within my stomach. I felt Solas' eyes on me as I struggled against the grip of Fae sickness. I hated him at that moment, more than any other Fae. If I could have, I would have cursed him. I'd have killed him with my bare hands.

* * * *

"Good morning, Perdi." Her voice called me out of a deep and restless sleep.

My arms were the first thing to scream out in pain. Searing agony radiated from my wrists to my armpits as if they had been splayed open and poorly stitched with iron. I flexed my hands and felt a stabbing and burning response from the muscles in my arms as they begged me not to do that again. I was weak, tired and dizzy, like I wanted to vomit, cry and sleep all at once. Emotions rolled over me in waves. Unable to choose just one to feel, I felt them all, with the very root being anger.

I pried my heavy eyelids open and winced at the brilliant light that instantly robbed me of my vision. Instinctively, I pulled my hand up to shield my face from the piercing sunlight. The movement made me flinch and lower my arms to the cold concrete floor. The chilled ground of wherever my kidnappers had shoved me, was also what calmed what my captors had done to me. I wanted to laugh—not because I found my situation funny but because I had been Taken again. There should be a rule somewhere that said I could only pay tithe once. I was sure that somewhere it had said I could only be a Crow for one realm at a time, and I was still serving my seven years.

I inched my eyes open a little at a time. My eyelids felt like sandpaper as they opened. Before I even sat up, I already knew I was in an iron cell. I could feel it press in on me, like sitting in a heated oven filled with sharp needles on all sides. I tried, in vain, to cast my magick, to feel where I was. But wards covered every inch of the room and stole my ability to use my magick freely. The walls were carved with symbols I had seen in the Darkmore journals. Small bags hung from the bars. One smell told me they were filled with herbs, roots and flowers Fae couldn't stomach. I sat in a Fae trap. It was as barbaric as I thought it would be.

From inside the cell, I couldn't feel Elphame, and my stomach twisted, cut off from the very world that now pumped my heart. I wondered how long I'd survive in a prison designed to kill me. I once thought I had understood what it felt like to be a Crow returned from Elphame. I didn't think it would take long before I went as mad as returned Crows once had when they were severed from Elphame. At least, when I went crazy from it, I wouldn't care anymore. I'd be too off my rocker to know what was happening. Here's hoping it would happen quickly, and this reality wouldn't matter in the end.

The woman who'd called my name was old as sin. She looked like every witch would, in the imaginations of children afraid of the dark. Her gray-and-stringy black hair was tied back, exposing her face. Everything about her appearance said the cookies she was serving weren't poisonous. But her eyes, the windows to her bitter old soul, said one bite would kill me. Through the bars, I felt her magick slink around her. She was a witch in the truest sense, not pure-blooded, but as evil as the rest of the charlatans in the mortal world. She was missing parts of a soul she had sold long ago to tinker with black magick. Alone, she was weaker than I was, but I doubted very much that only one witch was able to do this much damage. It would take a great many of them to work the kind of magick it took to pull me from Elphame.

"Good morning," I answered. I forced myself to sit up through the pain and the need to vomit and faced the wicked old bat. Although I was trapped, I didn't panic. I had been imprisoned before, and those who had done it were dead. So, I smiled at a dead woman who sat before me.

"My name is…" she started, and I interrupted her.

"I don't care who you are. I care why you've taken me and why you have done this," I asked and raised both arms to her. My anger dulled the pain enough for me not to pass out from it. It hurt like hell, but I was stubborn enough not to show her my discomfort. I had been sliced the length of my inner arms. I inspected the wounds and wondered if they had used iron and magick and if the cuts would scar me. I huffed a small laugh at my vanity. I was stuck in an iron hellhole, and I worried that it would leave a mark. "Why am I here?"

"My sisters and I have come to rebuild the Gate," she answered. "A Darkmore Gate needs Darkmore blood. As you can see from your arms, we've taken the blood we need."

"Good luck with that." I shook my head and tried not to laugh. Laughing in the face of captors would unlikely win me favors, but it was a chore not to. "There is nothing to rebuild."

"That is what you've claimed. But you, witch, will help us, or you will die."

"No, witch, I will not." I smiled wider. It wasn't a friendly smile. There was nothing funny about my situation, but fear always turned into anger for me. "And I doubt I'll be the one to die here. You will try, and you will fail. Just ask the bits and pieces of the Mages you sent to kill me. Their failure is scattered across our fields."

"Their sacrifice will not be forgotten. It got us here, didn't it? While you were busy hunting Mages and their fallout, we were setting the final Fae trap."

"I'm sure their last thoughts were of how noble their deaths were. What an honor that must have been for them when they were torn apart and eaten, never to return home again." I rolled my eyes. "You sent them to die, nothing more. There was no sacrifice, just a horrible death. And you're a damn fool to think dealing with the Fae will be any different for you. This—what you've done to me—will be the reason you die. Run along now, little witch. I won't be helping you today or any day."

"You'll change your mind, eventually," she replied. Her voice was as sure as water was wet. "You do not need to willingly help us to get what we've come for."

"If that's the case, why are you still talking?" I asked. "Why bother with these games?"

"To give you a chance."

"You have no idea how many were foolish enough not to kill me as soon as they had the chance. They all died in the end," I answered and stretched back onto the floor, closing my eyes. On the outside, I was cocky. On the inside, I was terrified. "You've bitten off more than you can chew, and I'll be there to watch your choke on it."

"My death doesn't scare me, child," she answered.

I raised my eyebrows, entertained by her stupidity, but didn't bother to look at her. "I'm glad. It'll make taking your heart easier and less messy. I hate having to chase people down."

"Would you sentence your people to the fate of Elphame? After all the Fae have done to them?"

"Yes," I answered. "If this is how Whitwick wishes to solve their problems, then this is how they will die. You, witch, are no better than the monsters you're scared of, if this is your idea of asking for help."

"You're a foolish and petty child."

"Oh, you have no idea how petty I can be," I answered. "Open the cage, and I'd be happy to show you, though."

"You will relive your Taking until you truly understand why we are doing this. You have forgotten all the Fae have done," the hag answered. "You have remembered only what you wish."

"I remember my Taking perfectly well, thank you," I replied. "Meeting the Fae leaves a mark no one forgets. There's not a day I don't remember."

"No, you do not. You do not remember how many traded their lives to protect their children, how many were brutalized at the hand of Fae. But you will remember."

"You're wrong. I remember every scream, every terror, every prayer for death. I remember them because I was there. You weren't. I screamed just as loud and prayed for death as everyone else did."

"And you wish for Whitwick to experience it again?" she asked.

I sighed. "Of course not."

"Then you understand why the Gate must return."

"And you need to understand that rebuilding the Gate is impossible," I answered. "Torturing me isn't going to give you what you want simply because you want it."

"Torturing you is not what we want. But if killing you gets us what we need, so be it," she answered with misplaced surety. "Your life is not more important than the lives of everyone else. The sooner you realize that, the easier this will be for you."

"How does it feel?" I asked.

"How does *what* feel?"

I rolled my head to her with a smile and stared her in the eyes. "To know you're going to die in the end?"

"You tell me," she asked and stood from her stool.

"Do your worst. I've lived the life of a Crow. You're not nearly creative enough for me to fear you." I finally laughed. "I'll tell you the same thing I told Elphame. You've Taken the wrong Crow, and I'll burn your world as I did theirs."

She stepped to the door and whispered. I didn't hear her words but felt the spell twist in the air and press down on my bones like a razor-sharp blanket. I didn't give her the pleasure of seeing me squirm, but inside my soul, I was screaming and begging for it to stop. It felt like being eaten by flames while freezing under a block of ice. My body couldn't figure out what was worse—the heat or the cold, being pulled apart or crushed.

"I will see you in a few hours, Perdi. By then, I hope you have changed your mind. This doesn't get harder for me, only you." She closed the door behind her.

I felt the first stir in my stomach and remembered the shadows had climbed down my throat. "Are you still here?"

"We're here…not all of us, though. You puked most of us up before you were Taken," they whispered back, and although I was in a world of pain, I relaxed a little, knowing I wasn't alone. Pain doesn't have the same edge to it when it's missing the fear of facing it on your own.

"Where the hell am I?"

"We are in the mortal realm," they replied. "We're in Whitwick."

"How are you here? How can you leave Zephyr?" I asked.

"We are bound to protect you. Zephyr heard the bells from inside Blood and Bones. He sent us to help you, no matter the cost."

"What happened?" I asked. "I remember being pulled from Blood and Bones, then hitting my head."

"A blood spell called you home."

"How did they get my blood?" I asked.

"We felt your father here when we crossed the Gate. We think they took him first, then used him to call you," they replied. "We know very little of your magick, but blood calls to blood, no matter what realm you're in."

My heart sank. "Is my dad still alive?"

"He was when we first got here. But now, we can't feel anything beyond this cage."

I curled my arms into my chest. "What have they done to me? Why the hell did they cut open my arms like this?"

"Blood, Perdi. They took as much blood as they could without ending your life. They performed a ritual with your blood. They were trying to call the Darkmore Gate. They believe they can rebuild the Gate with your soul and your magick. They have the original spell that called the Gate—or so that is what we have heard them say."

"They should have killed me," I muttered.

"They'd be safer if they had," they replied. "The stupid always die first."

"Will it work? What they're doing?"

"No, we don't believe so. If the witches were in Elphame, were of the original Sidhe, the rift of the Gate allowed it and had all the power of both realms, perhaps. But they're here…with you. All they can do from here is bleed you dry of your Elphame magick," they answered. "They will try and fail. Nothing is bringing that Gate back, but it won't stop them from believing they can. Fear makes a person believe just about anything."

"I dreamed of my Taking," I whispered. "I replayed it all."

"We know. We saw it, too," the shadows answered. "They want you to remember, to be angry and want to seek revenge for what was done. They think it'll convince you to help them, that you're remember something that'll make you hate the Fae."

"I didn't forget it," I replied. "It's not something I'm able to just forget. The life I have is because of that bloody Gate. Force-feeding me my Taking isn't going to make me hate anyone more than I'll hate them for doing it."

"This is true, but they feel you've forgotten the fear the others live in," they answered.

"I remember every time the Fae came. I've never forgotten my fear as I hid, praying they wouldn't come for me. Then they did," I answered. "And now, it's all twisted…the memories. I see parts I don't remember. There are parts added that I don't remember happening. I don't know if it's entirely real. It's as if they've warped it somehow, making it more perverse. It's like the truth, and my nightmares are mixed together. As if I needed that, to make me remember how bad it was."

"We were not there for your Taking. It is not something openly discussed. But we've been in your soul and your dreams, and what they're showing you isn't what your soul knows to be true," they answered. "They are twisting your mind with a curse, hoping you'll break under the fear of it. They're doing it so you fear Elphame."

"I *do* fear Elphame." I huffed a sarcastic laugh.

"We will do what we can to lessen it. But it is your soul who must remember the truth." They turned over and over in my stomach like they did not like being trapped inside. "Are you able to leave here?"

I looked at my cage and groaned. "I can't get out. It's warded. And even if I could, I don't think I'd get very far. They've taken too much blood. I'd be caught within minutes. Can *you* get out?"

"If you opened a small enough hole for us, we could try. But we wouldn't suggest it, Perdi. We cannot leave you like this. We are eating your pain. If we leave, this could very well kill you," they answered. "It is a very old Fae trap, and you are but a fledgling who is weak and untrained."

"Who the hell trains like this?" I asked but already knew the answer. "Zephyr does this to his people?"

"Yes. Not to the extent of bleeding them, as you've had done, but all Aos Si are trained to endure more torture than you'd ever survive. They have too many secrets not to be trained for every inevitability. If one were taken, they have to be able to die with those secrets," they replied. "But this — what is happening to you — is much worse. If we leave, you will feel it all, and we do not know if you're strong enough to withstand the pain of it."

"Staying here so that it doesn't hurt me as much doesn't do anything more than draw out my death. If we don't try, what was the point of you coming with me? So that I could endure more torture?" I answered. "Return to Elphame, tell them what's happening, tell them I need help."

The shadows began to roll around in jerky movements as if they were nervous. "What if you release a few of us and the rest remain? If too many of us leave and you die, what's the point of a rescue? You need to stay alive, or Solas and Zephyr are coming to claim a body."

"Would it work?" I asked. "What if the few of you don't make it? I won't be able to spell again. More need to leave, or there is no point going at all."

"A couple dozen of us will leave, but the rest will remain," they answered. "But know this, Perdi. It will hurt. It will hurt more than lashes, more than war. When we leave you, you'll feel all the spell that holds you and the cost of the spell to release us. We won't be able to protect you from all of it."

I nodded. "Everything hurts in the mortal world."

"There is no place for you in any realm where pain doesn't follow. That is the cost of power. You're noticed by all who want it for themselves," they answered. "We'll return with all of Elphame."

It had been years since I had needed to spell for anything, not life or death. Being in Elphame with wild magick flowing in the very air, I never needed to pay for the magick I used every day and had forgotten about the times before my Taking, when magick held a hefty cost for even the most mundane of things. The times I drew more power than usual, fate was there to remind me that greed hurt like hell. Spells always held a hefty cost that made fate shake her head at me. Today,

I'd pay dearly. I was too weak to not suffer for it. But I was too desperate not to try.

I curled onto my side and searched the floor for cracks and dips, a space where the Fae trap would be weaker. Without a weapon to slice my hand, I used my nails. Clawing your own hand is a harrowing experience. You instinctively pull away from the pain, but when you're doing it to yourself, your brain gets confused and tries to stop it from happening altogether. If you're not quick enough, you lose the nerve and need to start over. I ripped my flesh with my nails, cursed under my breath and ran the blood over a hairline crack in the cement. I pulled a few strands of hair from my head and closed my eyes. As I twisted my hair into knots, a rough witch's ladder, I whispered a spell. It felt awful to be using a Darkmore spell while sitting in a Fae trap designed by Darkmore witches. Fate had a sick sense of humor.

With knot one, my spell has begun.
With knot two, my heart is true.
With knot three, so mote it be.
With knot four, their spell can hold no more.
With knot five, the shadows shall thrive.
With knot six, this freedom spell is fixed.
With knot seven, their powers will not lessen.
With knot eight, this spell is my fate.
With knot nine, the cost is mine.
So mote it be.

The shadows didn't so much as fall from me as forcing their way up my throat. I vomited and gagged until they were free. I didn't have the chance to watch them leave. I passed out at the sheer force of the Fae trap they had been protecting me against. When payment came for the spell I had twisted to release the shadows, I was already writhing in pain. It didn't cost more than what was already racking my body. I was in and out and more thankful when I was unconscious. But as the shadows had warned, asleep only meant I didn't physically feel the pain. Emotionally, that was a different story. Memories that were not my own flooded my mind and twisted a different flavor of agony I was forced to suffer. When I clawed up and out of the darkness, I was faced with what felt like being skinned alive. Decisions, decisions. Asleep or awake, I suffered.

The moment I wished death would take me, the door opened. When the witch took her seat, the pain ended. I could almost thank her for the respite. Almost. I was vindictive enough to crawl back into the pain to spite her. I wasn't just petty. I was bitter and hateful.

"I felt your spell," she said.

"What did you expect? You locked a witch in a cage," I replied.

"You are no more a witch, Perdi. You gave that up when you chose to remain with our enemies. Every day you are in Elphame, you risk your human soul and your humanity." Her face held hate and disgust as if she had suffered with the rest of Whitwick. She had no idea what darkness she invited into these lands by bringing me to Whitwick. "The others wished to come and see what you had accomplished, but I doubted very much you could break the wards in this room. A Fae trap has never failed us. Had you been a witch and not Fae, as you claim, you'd be free from here."

"Nothing lasts forever," I answered.

"Forever is a long time to wait and see what lasts longest, you or the spell." Her grandmotherly voice made me glare through the bars at her. To hear such hate from someone who looked like they should be baking a cake made me hate her for the oddest of reasons. "Forever is a long time to run from the ghosts that haunt your mind."

I shrugged. "I come with a graveyard in my soul. If I couldn't deal with the ghosts, I'd have died long ago."

"Have you not wondered why you, a witch, would be spared?" she asked. "Why they didn't kill you?"

"Rest assured, I've been spared nothing."

"Perhaps they allowed you to live to keep the worlds between us open? Perhaps it is Darkmore blood that has kept the rift between worlds open?" she asked. "Why should we all suffer because you refuse to see you have become a tool for the Fae? Or perhaps it is you who wants the Gate to remain open?"

"My answer hasn't changed. No amount of torture is going to change reality," I replied. "There is no Gate to repair. It's gone. And this little spell of yours to call it back? There isn't enough power on this side of the Gate for that to happen. May I suggest we go to Elphame? I'm sure you'll find what you're looking for there."

"I do not believe you or the riddles of your kind," she answered, as if I were trying to talk circles around her. I wasn't. The truth was simply the truth in this case.

"Foolish hag," I countered. "There are three possibilities here, three likely paths we'll walk. First, there is no Gate to build, and there never will be another one. You will try and fail. The second, you believe you can bleed enough power from me to call the Gate. You have me warded, which means the endless well of energy I receive from Elphame is drying up. So, we're back to you trying and failing."

"And the third?" she asked.

"It is what *will* happen." I smiled at the fate I knew she'd face one way or another. "You and your sisters will die here. I believe whatever path is walked, you all die in the end. You will have failed and given your life for a lost cause. I hope selling your soul for dark magick was worth it."

"No, Perdita. *You* will be the one who dies. But first, with your blood, we'll close Whitwick off from Elphame."

"I once wished you luck in your pursuit. Now, I simply wish for your death. Slow or quick, I'm really not that picky." I let the laughter bubble out of me. "Mark my words, witch. Those who have stood against me before, I left their bodies splayed for the birds, just as I will do to you."

The pain took over as she whispered. Her voice brought the weight of the world crashing onto my chest. Darkness, thankfully, came hard and fast, and the pain was over. I rested in between deep sleep and fully awake. Just enough to hear the world around me but not enough to be bothered by it. I stayed in the safety of my shadowy sleep, with the shadows holding me deep within. But inside that slumber, I relived every moment of my Taking, from when the Gate opened to the time I was Taken back into Whitwick. The shadows had a choice. They either kept me awake enough to feel the pain of the cage or sleeping deep enough to feel the pain of my Taking. Emotional pain was the lesser of two evils when physical pain would keep me a victim in a world that wanted me to bleed for them. So, I relived it, over and over. But after hours of it, it wasn't the lesser. I'd rather be dead than remember.

Each new memory showed me glimpses into the coming of Fae, moments in time I hadn't noticed or refused to see. Fresh blood under the nails of Faolan.

Drops of blood on the front of Solas' dress shirt. A terrified Nix, who struggled between the lies he told and the truth he so desperately wanted to say to me. And I hurt all over again. Long-healed scabs tore off, and I bled for being a Crow…again.

Chapter Four

The only sounds were of my ragged breathing and the shuffling of feet over gravel. My near-lifeless body swayed over the shoulder of a man. He smelled of farm and wine and iron. My arms dangled down his back, wet and sticky, throbbing in constant pain. I was heavy and weightless at once, as if I were already dead and waiting for death to come to collect my body. It was calmer than the last time I'd kissed my demise on the lips. Today I didn't feel the panic of survival, the need to fight tooth and nail for a beating heart. I didn't feel much of anything aside from the aches of wounds still raw and unhealed. There was a quiet acceptance found in life's final moments, an understanding of what was coming and knowing fate would be stronger than I was this time. Of all the reasons for my death I thought I'd have, I did not think becoming a mortal Crow would be the cause of my grave.

The scent of a horse filled my nose. In my daze, I braced myself for what I knew would happen once I was placed on that horse. The man slid me off his shoulder onto the rear of the horse. I wasn't on for more than a few seconds before I was bucked off onto the sharp stones and sticks of the earth. The jarred landing brought me swimming back up from my deathbed. The man gripped my arms as my eyes flew open, and I, in turn, reached for him. The knife hanging off his belt was in my hand within the blink of an eye. I pulled him onto me and pushed the knife into his throat. I wrapped my legs around him, locking him into place as I held his face into my chest. He didn't have the chance to scream, but I was prepared to silence the slightest whisper. The warm rush of blood coated my hand and body as he twitched his final moments on top of me. There were dozens of moments, lives I had taken, that I had regretted. This man would not be one of them. There was no remorse in me. The moment he helped torture me, he gave up his right to live.

I pulled the knife out of the man's neck and pushed him off me. I slowly stood and regretted the quick movement. The world spun, and if it weren't for my stomach being empty, I'd have been sick. I dragged the still-bleeding body from the path and rolled him into a patch of high weeds and grass. I grabbed his bag and left my prison behind. I gripped the knife, feeling my chance of survival had increased with the addition of a weapon. How greatly those chances improved was yet to be seen. I may have been walking from one prison to a grave, but I would be taking others to that hole with me.

As much as I wanted to head back toward the Gate and the possibility of returning to Elphame, I knew I'd have been captured once again. I was too weak to fight and too depleted to survive another attack. Away from Whitwick, I headed. I ran the best I could with the bit of energy I had. I was empty of everything but my will to live. Under the light of the moon, I maneuvered through the back hills of Whitwick and into the forest beyond. I had to get as far away from those who hunted me while it was still dark enough to stay hidden. I needed time to recover if I ever wanted a chance in hell of escaping the mortal realm. Every step was a balance between life and death. I was weak and dizzy, and each movement was too swift for my brain to follow. I fell, dry heaved and cried out in pain and uncertainty, but I still got back up. To stay down would mean death. Giving up wasn't an option.

I felt the magick prickle down my spine before I could stop my feet from taking another step. My sluggish heart pounded as my ears began to ring. The world tilted, and the hair on my arms sizzled. I turned to go a different route and hit a wall of glass. It felt like a bolt of lightning struck down, and I was lifted off my feet and blown through the air. My vision swam the moment I hit the ground. The darkness came fast and hard, and I was out cold. I usually welcomed being knocked out, but tonight the thought terrified me.

* * * *

My dream of Solas dragging me by the hair toward the Gate shattered to the sound of crows. I woke to the warmth of the sun, fresh air and no cage around me. I lifted my heavy arm to block the light from my eyes and slapped myself as it fell. My arm felt like iron filled my bones. I tried to push my magick into the air around me but drew on an empty tank. The fear began to slide in at the edge of my mind, shoving my grogginess away. The realization that I wasn't in Elphame sank in, and I groaned. I was still in the mortal realm. Was it too much to ask to be rescued and not have to be the one doing the rescuing? While lying face up to the sun and cooking off the dregs of energy I would need to keep my heart beating, it clearly was an ask too great.

I pulled on my training but moved slower than I had ever been in the forest with Solas or Zephyr. I knew I had to protect myself. I needed a weapon. Without one would keep me a victim. I had to get up. I needed cover. Being out in the open made me a target. Instead of doing all I was trained to do, I stayed on my back and paid closer attention to my heart skipping beats as fear coursed through my veins.

On the ground for the birds to pick me clean, growing weaker by the minute, I wouldn't be able to defend myself should the need arise. And I doubted very much that the need wouldn't come. I was too sore and too depleted of magick and energy. Yet, it boiled down to two choices, regardless of my condition or wants or needs, I could lie there and rot in the sun or save myself. I seriously debated the rotting part. It would have been so much easier than anything else I knew I'd have to do, and it would likely hurt less. But survival instincts didn't always listen to the scared parts of your brain. The need to survive usually won out over the need to lie there and take it. But it would have been nice, for once, to not have to wrestle my fear into submission. How grand that would be to live a life I didn't have to fight for.

"Welcome home, Crow," I muttered. My dry throat seized around each word, and I coughed on them. Five years and change, and my Crow membership would expire. If it didn't get any better than this, the relentless risk to my life, I'd need to be caged or killed. I doubted my grip on my morality or sanity would last if I had five more years of this still to come. I was hoping for the death part. The dead don't care about such things as wars. The dead didn't suffer, either.

With a stranglehold on my fear, I forced myself to shut the door to my willingness to give up. I was almost sad when the door closed and I decided to fight. Although I knew that one day I'd wake up and this would be behind me, that the weight of another Taking would be a distant memory I didn't want, it still pissed me off that I was here to begin with. I smiled for a moment. The thought that I'd die here was gone. The only emotion left behind was that I'd be ticked off when it was over. Giving up had only been a fleeting thought. I was either getting braver or the sun had already cooked my brain, and I was delirious.

Begrudgingly, I moved my body against every need to remain still. It felt like I had been running for days, swimming for hours and hadn't eaten in weeks. I was cramped and water-logged. With my link to Elphame cut off, I felt with more than my magick, with parts that I was only just relearning how to depend on. I focused on my other senses. I was lying on rough grass, the kind that grew in the hills and hadn't been tended to by hand. It was the same grass I remember running through as a child. It would poke and stab and scratch. That alone told me I was far from town, away from the people who still cared about their lawns. I could smell the earth, rich and musty, untainted by trash or people. Overhead, the sky and treeline were filled with birds' songs. I had to be far enough from the Gate to hear birds. They didn't like being near the power of Elphame. When I was a child and hunted the forests, I had to walk for hours before the barest hint of wildlife could be found.

I opened my eyes and let them adjust to the blazing sun, afraid of what I'd see. I was scared I'd wake from a dream and still be locked in that cage, bombarded by memories corrupted to terrify me more than the truth already had. Instead, I was in a field surrounded by trees. I couldn't feel Elphame, not even a murmur of it. I couldn't feel anything more than pain. I whispered to the shadows, but nothing returned — silence inside, no voices around me, no light hum of magick. I tried for my Malice but felt nothing. I couldn't remember the last time I was truly alone. My Malice had been a constant since I could remember. The shadows were always near and a call away. Solas was always close by, and Zephyr was a thought away. Nix could usually be found around any corner and had his ear tuned to my voice at all times. Nix could sense me from across the realm and come before my first tear fell. And lately, the Aos Si followed me around like my own casted shadows.

It was an unusual feeling to be alone with my thoughts, alone with my dread and fear. What made it worse was that I was in Whitwick. That I was uncertain about my survival in a place that I had once called home shattered any hope I held out for finding peace between both realms. The one place I had fought so hard to get back to was the very place I feared waking up in. How quickly life had changed for me to wake up scared to be in the mortal realm.

I rolled to my side and winced against the burn that radiated throughout my muscles and joints. Nausea watered my mouth and teared my sight. I bit my cheek to keep myself from screaming out in pain. All my skin felt raw and scabbed over. There wasn't an inch of my body, inside or out, that didn't feel like it had been boiled. I tried to push myself to my feet, but my legs and arms felt like I had spent hours swimming against a current. I wasn't just drained of energy in the way hours of training wore me out. I had literally been drained of blood until my heart struggled to beat to a tune I would consider normal. Each time I moved too fast, my chest hurt, and my lungs and heart strained under the demand. I was tired, both physically and emotionally drained, as though I hadn't slept in days. My muscles were cramped like I had lifted well beyond my limit and didn't stop when they started to tear. I glanced down at my arms. My skin was pale, almost sickly gray, and every freckle and wound stood out in stark contrast. I stared at my nail beds, which were no longer pink, and was surprised the witches hadn't pulled out my nails to make me help them do the impossible.

Even though I had been lying in the sun, I still shivered. I wondered if Fae went into shock from losing too much blood. I knew humans did, and it happened very quickly. I was somewhere in the middle, between human and Fae. How long would it take for me to die from a great many things plaguing me on this fine, sunny day? Infection, blood loss, magick starvation, weakness, dehydration or being hunted down again. I hoped I wouldn't find out, but I wouldn't hold my breath. The mortal world didn't steal me into Whitwick, drain and torture me for me to live through it. They'd eventually try to finish the job, because that's what I would do. If my enemy got away, I'd regroup and hunt them down. I had a feeling the people of Whitwick were as spiteful as I am. One look at my arms told me they were as hateful.

I gave up trying to stand. My legs refused to work just yet. The pins and needles were still rolling up and down my limbs, working to regain their blood supply. That the tingling was still here after several minutes made me nervous about the lack of blood in my body. Instead of fighting against numb legs, I focused on my surroundings and gaining my bearings. It took more time than it should have to concentrate, to make sense of what I was seeing around me. At my side, a backpack, covered in bright red splashes of blood, just like my hands and spatters on my clothes. A distant memory surfaced of me being carried from my prison. I was being moved—for what and to where, I didn't know. A guard, who had helped hold me down while I was tortured repeatedly, had carried me to a horse. Horses never liked Fae, and I was bucked off. When I landed on my side, barely feeling the pain of it, over everything else I had already suffered, it jarred me from my wounded sleep. It pushed me out of my willingness to let go of my life. When the guard attempted to pick me up, I'd taken his life and gear and run. I'd come through a wall of wards, and my attempt to leave had been met with brutal force, and I'd passed out when I hit the ground.

Where they had held me was on the outskirts of Whitwick, far enough away for the locals to not hear my screaming. And where I was now, I didn't know. Nothing looked familiar. It wasn't Whitwick, but it was mortal lands. Wherever this glass cage was, I had never been. The hills were unfamiliar, the mountain range I couldn't place. The earth felt and smelled similar to Whitwick, but nothing appeared to be the same. But I was a halfling. I never went this far away from home. It was close enough to feel like home but far enough away for me not to be a threat. I wondered why a warded cage had been placed in the middle of nowhere. You only caged those you were terrified of. That thought jolted my panic. I had locked myself into a bubble of whatever scared the witches. I had run from a certain death to a likely one. That was enough for me to convince my body to move.

I crawled on quivering arms and legs that felt like jelly from the cooking sun into the shade. Although I was cold, and it felt better to be in the sun, I didn't want to risk sunstroke. I didn't need to burn off my skin any more than I wanted to sit in the gloom of the trees, but I'd hate to find my will to live only to die from something so common and human. I rifled through the bag, fighting against dizzy spells, and found the guard's lunch, a jug of water and some fruit. My hands trembled as I slowly ate an apple and drank the water. I poured a little water on my hands to wash off the blood, but I was covered in it, most of which I doubted came from the guard I had killed. The apple hit my stomach like a brick, and I fought not to bring it back up. It soured and turned in my clenched stomach. I couldn't remember the last time I had eaten. One apple filled me to the point I thought I'd be sick.

Weak or not, I had to find cover and get out of the open before nightfall. Never mind whatever lurked in my surroundings… I had killed a guard to get away. Either someone had to be looking for me or already knew where I was and would take my life just as fast as whatever creatures would be coming out as soon as dusk set in. I waited until the nausea passed before moving again. It felt like I had rested for hours, trying to convince myself to muster. Each moment dragged out longer than the last. My sluggish pulse thumped randomly in my ears and reminded me how very human I now was. I laughed at the twist of fate I had been given. I paid tithe to the Gods of Elphame, fought wars and clawed my way back from the brink of death on more than one occasion. And now I'd die because I bled too much in the very world I had been stolen from and once prayed I'd come back to. I'd gotten what I asked for. I came back, and I was mortal once again. I glanced up at the sky and cursed our God. It was a deadly twist of fate.

I crawled on the prickly grass and rocks, sluggish and uncoordinated. Anyone who wanted to find me could track the little bits of flesh I left behind on the matted grass. I remembered Zephyr telling me to leave no trace behind, and as I looked back, I could see the path I was gouging into the earth. I slinked on the ground until the apple had given me enough strength to stand, although standing was not what I did. I shuffled. I shook. I swayed in the light breeze as if it held the force of a storm. I gripped anything stronger than I was to keep myself upright. From tree to tree, I made my way along the edge of the field I had awoken in, stopping at each new tree until vertigo and nausea faded. I couldn't risk getting sick. One look in my pack had told me I didn't have enough food or drink to replace what would come back up. A few apples and a sweet bar wouldn't keep me going for long.

Along the way, I picked berries and roots Nix had taught me I could eat. I could almost hear Nix's voice, showing me how to tell the difference between what could sustain me and what would take my life. We had spent countless hours in the back hills of Whitwick, camping, fishing, hunting and living off the land. I was thankful for those days, regardless of how much I hated this realm now. Those years would be how I'd survive today.

I passed the horse nettle, with its tempting tomato-looking fruits, and gave a wide berth to the giant hogweed. Fruits and berries that would kill me or blister my skin were left on their vines where they belonged. There were quicker ways to die than poison. Eating toxic plants would be a long and painful way to go. I nibbled on whatever I could find and keep down that wouldn't induce a horrible death, then collected more for later — if there was a later for me. I didn't like my odds, although they were better than they had been just the previous day.

I wasn't as sluggish as I had been when first opening my eyes, but I was moving excruciatingly slowly. The juices and sugars from the handful of berries gave me the boost I needed to keep moving forward, but ants marched faster than I was. If I wanted a chance at living through this, I had to regain my strength again and couldn't depend on magick. I had survived almost eighteen years without spooling Elphame magick in my soul. I could do it again. I remembered Aeden telling me that the Aos Si did not use Fae magick. This must be why. It could be taken away too quickly.

Zephyr had trained all his people to live in the conditions I was currently standing in. I had balked at his training and now wished I had gone every day. The times I did go would serve me well. But I'd have given a few toes to know what I had missed on the days I didn't go. Between him and Nix, I had a chance, and that was all I needed. That's all I had ever needed. I knew what my priorities were and walked until the sun began to set, away from the field and into the shadows of the surrounding forest. I never used to fear the dark, but now I don't like it. It rolled down my spine and mixed with my memories and fresh fears. The dark reminded me of the inside of a casket, and I felt like I was close to climbing into it.

I inspected a small cavern of roots and rock and decided it looked like a great place to die. It was empty and as secure as it would get for me. I dragged bits of wood and moss into what once was a treed hill. The collapse of the root system had created a small cave in the rear that was free from the eyes of anyone who would be hunting me. The walk to the back of my new dirt hovel didn't feel like finding a safe place to sleep. It reminded me that I was on my own—scared, hunted, hurt—and could become a victim again at the drop of a hat.

Tucked into the back, starting a fire took me longer than ever before. My hands refused to work, and I smashed my knuckles with a rock more times than the rocks connected with each other. Once I got my small fire going, I calmed down a little more. The fire would do nothing to protect me, but it chased away the darkness. If anything, it would give away my location, but I couldn't risk freezing to death. Although the weather had been warm, nights in Whitwick got cold, and my body was in no condition to heat itself through to the morning. *Decisions, decisions. Die from being found or die from exposure.* I'd take my chances and stay warm.

Under the light cast by my small fire, I examined my body for injuries and infection. Each arm had healing slices from armpit to wrist, and I wondered how I didn't just bleed out from those wounds alone. I had been stitched shoddily. The skin was puckered in places, and I knew I wouldn't heal nicely from it. Solas had once told me when wounds didn't heal properly, they'd have to be recut and healed again. He had many from battles that had been stitched together on the field, and he'd had to reopen them at home and sew them back together. The thought wasn't appealing. If I made it home in one piece, I was guessing I'd be in for another round of torture just to heal my arms.

Beyond the slices down my arms, I felt raised scabs of healing wounds. I inched closer to the fire to see small symbols had been carved into my flesh. I lifted my shirt and rolled up my pants. From head to toe, the witches had marked my body. They were no bigger than a coin in some places and the size of my hand in others. I didn't know all of them but recognized the ones we had carved on our doors long ago to protect us from the Fae. They had placed Fae wards on a Fae. *How utterly disgusting*. I ran my fingers over the marks and felt them flare up under my touch, pulling on the energy I had left. The symbols were what was blocking my Fae abilities and the very magick I'd use to help rid my body of them. Without magick to help me break the wards on my flesh, I had no choice but to use a knife to cut their power from my skin. I cringed at the realization that I'd have to injure myself even more than I already was.

"And *we're* the monsters?" I muttered to myself and snorted a small laugh. I had stopped considering myself a mortal around the same time mortals started to think of me as Fae. I may have felt very human at this moment, but I wasn't.

I dug the only knife I had out of the bag, and with a piece of wood between my teeth, I sliced the first symbol on my leg, ending its magick. It hurt worse than I thought it would. I swallowed my scream and snapped the wood held between my teeth. When the spell broke, I dropped the knife and cursed the witches. As the magick left through my freshly bleeding wound, my body was washed over in blistering heat. I stared at the knife and didn't want to touch it again. But if I didn't remove them, I'd keep growing weaker. I was too Fae to have these symbols on my flesh and not pay a hefty consequence for them. I had no choice but to slice them open. Until they were gone, any magick I tried to use would either end my life or be nullified by the wards on my body. Empty of Elphame, I could do nothing more than I was born with, which came at a price I couldn't pay tonight...bleeding out. I couldn't risk slicing too deep and spilling the little blood I still had left. Tonight, not a drop could be spared. Exhaustion tugged at my mind. I put my knife away and would start again tomorrow in the daylight.

I curled onto my side and replayed everything I could remember from my Taking into Whitwick. It was broken and jumbled. A fog I couldn't shake from my mind created gaps in my memories. Events played out in random order like a storm had ripped pages from a book and left behind a chaotic mess to pick through. I remembered voices, pain, sleep and repeat—demands to help construct a Gate that I didn't know how to build, whispers of killing me to do it. Each time I refused, more pain, more screaming, more bleeding. They accused me of being foolishly brave, but it wasn't bravado. I simply couldn't do what they wanted, even if I wanted to. Had there been a way to create a Gate, I'd have done it long ago when I was first asked to do it. The threat of death didn't make it any more possible, but it did make me unwilling to hear their plight or care for their safety. They'd forfeited my bleeding heart for them the moment they'd taken me from my home. I drifted off to thoughts of revenge and freedom. I would have both before I returned to Elphame. I was that petty and that hateful.

Chapter Five

I jerked from a restless sleep to a faint noise, almost too light to hear. I wondered if I had taken someone else's hiding spot or, worse, the home of a bear. Faintly, I heard small leaves crunch, followed by what sounded like someone biting into an apple. Bears, to my knowledge, didn't tiptoe around at the mouth of a cave or warm themselves by a fire. Bears were scavengers. They didn't care if they disturbed your sleep and wouldn't pass up a wounded person for an apple.

"Who's there?" I asked, and the noise stopped. I could hear feet shuffle to the opening of the cave. "Wait, please. I won't hurt you. I need help."

"There is no help I can give you. We are the cursed," he replied but paused at the cavern door.

A laugh burst from my mouth. "I don't know if you've noticed, but I'm a walking curse myself. I have been since the day I was born. Please, just tell me where I am and the direction of Whitwick Gates."

"For most, perhaps a week's walk if you follow the river down. For you, I do not think you'd make it. You smell of rot and worse things. But the point is moot. These lands are warded. No one can get in or out."

"I got in, and you got in. There's obviously a way out," I replied and sat up. I wanted to reach through the darkness to him. I didn't want him to leave me alone.

"We are brought here, but no one ever leaves," he answered.

"Where the hell am I?"

"Several miles from the back border of Whitwick Gates. You're on cursed land, and I suggest you do a better job at hiding before the cursers find you. They always come to kill survivors when they get bored."

"They've warded me. I doubt they could find me if I stay out of sight," I replied.

"It is your fire that gives you away. You're too close to the warded wall. The cursers will see the light from your fire," he replied. "If you want to survive, put out your fire. Tomorrow, move up the hills into the trees. You'll be safer and out of sight."

"Please don't leave me," I whispered when I heard him move again. "Please, don't go."

"Who are you?" he asked.

"My name is Perdita Darkmore."

"Perdi?" His voice raised. "You're alive?"

I heard him shuffle back to the rear of the cave, where I sat curled in a ball. He was nude, and where wings once stood proudly, small scarred stumps remained. He *had been* a fairy until they took away his wings. He ran around the rocks and frantically up my front to my face. His tiny hands grabbed my cheeks, and he hugged my chin. With apple-scented lips, he kissed me.

"Oh, Perdi." He hugged me tighter. "We thought you were dead. We all thought you were gone. You smell different now. I didn't know it was you."

"Do I know you?" I asked.

"My apologies, I forgot myself." He jumped from my front and dipped his head with a smile. "I'm one of Orrian's people, Carver. We met in the forest when you were on the run from the Golden Court and again at your birthday. I am one of Orrian's sentries. I have been guarding your home since the day you came into the Dark Courts."

"What have they done to you?" I whispered and reached for his shoulders but didn't touch where his wings once stood. Fresh tears dripped from my eyes. "Your wings... What have they done?"

"I didn't give them anything, Perdi. Even as they took my wings, I didn't tell them about you. I stared them in the eyes and didn't utter a word. They thought me to be weak. But I'd have rather died, suffered worse than the loss of my wings, than tell them how to hurt you, how to force you."

"You sacrificed your wings for me?" My chin quivered. "Oh, Carver, I'm so sorry. You should have just told them what they wanted to hear. Maybe they wouldn't have done this to you."

He pushed his shoulders straighter and lifted his head. Somehow, he looked braver, taller, even in the dark, without his wings, covered in marks and a smattering of healing scars. "And leave you to suffer in my place? You'd never do that to any of us. Why would we do that to you? I would sooner meet my death with honor and pain than buy myself an extra day, to die in shame and bring my clan dishonor. My pearl would never be worthy of being carried into the arms of the

Goddess without sacrifice. When it is my time to go, the Goddess will collect me herself and will give me back my wings."

I nodded, although I didn't entirely agree with his logic. I'd have suffered for him, even if he only got one extra day with his wings. But the wee folk had pride and honor. They were the first to battle and the last to leave. "What happened, Carver? How did you get here?"

"I came through the Gate weeks ago after you went missing. Orrian sent scouts, everyone did. But those sent through rarely returned. When they took me, they drained me of my magick. And when they were done with me, they cursed me to live out my days, they said, as mortal."

"Weeks? How long have I been here?" I asked.

"About a month."

"A month?" I whispered. "It only feels like a couple of days, at most."

"Time moves differently when you're being tortured," he answered. "For some, it's a blink. For others, they feel every second and movement through time as if it were a crawl. Once they've taken our magick, they dump us here in the cursed lands."

"Why are they taking our magick?" I asked.

"They're spooling Fae magick to build a Gate, to seal off Elphame for good."

I remembered what King Theofanis had said before he'd met his fate. Someone had taught the mortals how to steal our magick. I had thought the threat was against me and that they'd try to kill only me. Instead, all Fae would suffer for a Gate that would never be built.

"How many of our people are here?" I asked.

"Hundreds have landed on this soil, but only a couple dozen of us have survived beyond the theft of our magick. Most go mad and die. Some just whither overnight." His voice was soft. It held the pain of those I knew he had watched suffer and die. "Us wee folk seem to live longer. You're only the second larger one to survive."

"We need to get out of here," I replied. "We need to find a way to get back to Elphame."

"I would like nothing more than to return home, Perdi, but how? Those who have tried to cross the wards have died. We are cursed to remain on these lands until we die."

"We have to try," I answered.

"You are empty of Elphame. I can smell it. How do we try when all of us are as you are?"

"You were born of Elphame. I wasn't," I replied. "I was born a witch, born into this mortal world. That is how we try. But we can't do it if we're weak. Can we trade aid?"

"I have nothing to give you, I'm afraid."

"But you do. I need you to find the wards on my body. I can't reach them all and can't do a spell with them on me. Even if I could do it myself, I don't think I could cut myself that many times without passing out. Bite them, just enough to break their hold," I answered. "Whatever blood is drawn is yours to keep. The blood will give you the strength you need."

"Then what?"

"I do the same for you. We're not cursed. We're warded," I answered.

"Then we can leave?" he asked.

"The wards on our bodies, I think, are to keep us here, to keep us from Elphame magick, to guard us against using our abilities," I replied. "If we can find the others and do the same for them, hopefully we can leave this place and go home."

"Escape? We will certainly die before we ever reach the Gate," he answered.

"Then those who took us will die with us," I answered matter-of-factly. "I'd rather die trying to get home with my hands covered in witch's blood, than rotting in the back of this cave. If we are fated to die in the mortal world, we'll paint their streets red with their blood on our way out."

"I see why Orrian is so fond of you. You would have made a good fairy."

"Thank you. I take that as a huge compliment." I smiled. "Will you help me?"

"Perhaps you do me first, then the blood I take from you will help me heal and remain on guard while you're unconscious," he suggested. "You, I'm afraid, will likely pass out from the pain. It will hurt—our bite always does—and there's nothing I can offer you to take that away."

"Physical pain doesn't scare me, Carver," I answered, but I still shuddered at the thought of his teeth sinking into my flesh.

"These marks… You're sure I won't die if you cut them?" he asked. "We've all seen them but have been too scared to remove them."

"I've already cut one and I'm still alive, so I think it's safe to assume they haven't marked us with anything like that. I don't think they have the power to curse us in such a way or we'd all be dead. We'd have died the moment they marked us."

"Why didn't they just kill us?" he asked softly, as if afraid of the answer. "When they were done with us, why not just take our lives? Why put us here?"

"It isn't much of a punishment if we're dead, is it? It isn't fun unless we're screaming." My mind flashed back to Solas, carrying me into the dungeon, telling me it wasn't a punishment if I passed out from the pain, then dumped me in a cell. And he was right. It was a night I'd never forget. I shook the memory to the bottom of my mind and locked it away to deal with when I wasn't about to shave off my flesh for this hellhole.

"You smell sad," Carver whispered.

"This is my second Taking," I answered. "I'm still not a fan of it."

"This is the fourth time I've been held captive, and it's no better than the first time. Although, it's the first time I've not had my wings, and I, too, am not a fan." He turned his back to me. "Let's get this over with."

I nodded and pulled out my knife. I held just the very tip. I closed my eyes and felt every inch of Carver's skin. There were only four. He wasn't big enough for more. I nicked each one just enough to spill blood, cleanse the wound and break the ward. He didn't flinch or fight not to scream as I had. When the spell broke and radiated his body with pain, he made no move against it. It made me sadder to know it didn't hurt as much as what he had already endured. Four small knicks and a wave of power from the broken wards were nothing compared to having his wings cut from his body.

"I'll kill them for what they've done to you," I whispered, more as a promise to myself than to him.

"Staying alive and getting you home is more important than my revenge. That can come later after you're safe." He cleaned the dribbles of blood from his body, then turned to me. "I don't know about this, Perdi."

"Just do it," I answered. "Please."

"Wait. I'll be right back." Carver jumped from me.

"Wait, no. Please. Don't leave me here, please," I begged. "Don't go."

He turned. "I'll come back. I swear. I didn't come this far just to leave you behind once I've found you."

Fear crept in the moment I was alone again, and my already tired heart started to pound. The knife clanged against the ground, and I jumped at the noise I had made. My hands were trembling and sweaty. I picked the knife back up, cursing myself for being so weak. I hadn't shaken the fear still in my bones from dreaming of the same terrors over and over. Every time I closed my eyes, it was all I saw and felt, right down to the smells surrounding me. I was bombarded with thoughts of the day that changed everything for me. I shook my head in hopes of shaking the memories to the bottom. But being alone didn't help my cause, and the anxiety roared back to life.

"Perdi?" Carver called from the mouth of the cave. "I have someone with me. Don't be scared. He's with us and is big enough to help me."

"Who is it?" I asked.

"It's me…Finn."

"Finn?" I called out. "*My* Finn?"

His soft laugh rolled through the darkness. "Yes, *your* Finn."

I watched as Carver darted back into the cave. His little shadow danced along the wall. Behind him, a hulk of a man who consumed every spare space moved through the rock and root room. He was too big for the cave and had to duck. His shadow ate up the walls and darkened every inch. I backed up. My mind raced between nightmares and reality. I was bombarded with memories, some real, some made to feel real and others made up. I didn't know what to believe as my mind whirled. They felt real, regardless of how true they were. And the closer he got, the more I wanted to run.

Trapped.

Prey.

Fae.

Taking.

I shook my head from side to side. "No, no, no, no…"

"Perdi." Finn grabbed me, and I froze under his touch. His hug felt foreign, uncomfortable. "God, I'm so glad to see you. I thought you were dead." He paused, feeling me shake under his touch. "It's okay. You're safe. You're not trapped. I'm not here to hurt you. You're safe with me. I swear to you, I'm your friend."

I nodded. "I'm sorry. I'm…"

"Scared," he finished my sentence. "It's okay to be scared."

"It's okay, Perdi," Carver called from my side. "Just breathe. Finn is our friend. He will help you."

I told myself to relax, that no matter what my twisted mind told me, Finn wasn't the one who walked the streets with the fog. He hadn't come for my Taking. Finn didn't dump me in Elphame. He wasn't my enemy. I told myself that it didn't matter either way…not right now. I needed help more than I needed to convince myself that he wasn't responsible for my suffering. I didn't need to trust the tools at hand.

"How are you here?" I asked. "I mean, *why* are you here?"

"I came in after you, before the Gate closed," he answered. "I chased after you and came through seconds after they took you. I didn't let go of your hand."

"They captured you?" I asked.

"Yes, with an iron sack and a rock bigger than my head," he replied. "I never hold a reserve of Elphame power, since I rarely use it, so the witches used me up within weeks. I've been here, within the warded world, for almost two weeks."

"You look…like you just got here." I tilted my head and stared at him. He looked as he always did, and nothing like having just spent two weeks in some torture chamber then being dumped in this hell hole. "You look rested, oddly fresh in some way."

"I didn't suffer as others did. They couldn't do anything to me that hasn't already been done many times before. We train for this, for years upon years — decades of this shit in preparation for moments like this. A few weeks with the witches was not worse than training," he answered and settled in front of me. "This isn't the first time I've felt this level of hate. I told you once before, it would take many years for my captors to stomach what it would take to end my life. And what they've got isn't nearly enough. All they've managed to do is piss me off, then plunk me into the middle of a forced vacation."

"I don't know if I should be sad that you've experienced worse or glad that Zephyr had the forethought to train you in this," I answered.

"Be glad. I certainly am," Finn answered. "What about you? You smell like..."

"Please don't." I cut him off. "I know what I smell like. I can feel it. I don't want to talk about what happened with them, please."

"I was going to say you smelled like a warm bag of gnome shit, but very well," he joked. "I can't tell you how relieved I am that you're alive."

I nodded. "Did Carver tell you about the wards?"

"Yes. We've been wondering about them, but none of us know anything about the craft of witches and didn't want to risk touching them. It is why Carver came for me. He says he's scared you'll pass out when he bites you."

"Carver, I would have been okay."

He shook his head. "No, I don't think you would be. Not only is my bite painful, but ridding your body of this magick will make it worse for you. And if you pass out, I won't be able to protect you from any who may come. The smaller Fae, yes. But what if the cursers were to show up? I'm not big enough to do anything to help you. I have no wings, Perdi, and no magick. I would fail you."

"You wouldn't fail. You'd do everything you could—and that's not a failure," I answered but nodded. I understood what he meant but hated the reason he felt powerless. Without his wings, he felt like he was lesser than he'd once been. I could relate. I was half a Crow without my magick. "All right, let's do this. After me, we'll do you, Finn."

"Can I pick the knife? Sorry, Carver, but I've been bitten by your kind before. Stings like a bit— Sorry, Perdi."

"No, it's okay. It *does* sting like a bitch," I answered. "I've been chewed on by Orrian. It's not a pleasant experience."

"Why the hell would you let a fairy chew on you?" Finn asked.

"My first night in the Golden Court, I was lashed for being too brave. Orrian came to my prison cell afterward and chewed off the infection," I replied.

"Dear God." Finn visibly cringed. "All right, then, let's do this. I can use the knife on you, if you'd prefer that over teeth? Or we can both go at it and get it done faster?"

"Both of you. Let's just do it and get it over with. It's going to hurt, and I'd rather it be done as quickly as possible," I answered. "Unlike you, I've never suffered decades of torture. I'm not used to it."

Carver jumped from my thigh. "I'm sorry, Perdi, but you must get undressed. We will do as you've asked, but I do not have the ability to keep the pain from you. Our bite is small, but it is searing."

Finn turned his head and covered his view of me undressing. "Sorry, Perdi. If it makes you feel any better, I'd rather not see you naked."

"Thank you?" I huffed a laugh.

"No, I mean, I'd like to see you naked, but Zephyr and Solas are going to pull out my eyes for this," he replied, then groaned. "I don't mean I want to see you naked because I don't. I mean, it's not a fate worse than death, but it's not something I'd like to go blind for. I'm just going to stop talking because I'm making it worse."

I laughed at his awkwardness. "It's okay. I know what you mean. If Zephyr or Solas have a problem with it, you can stand behind me, and I'll protect you." I pulled off the rest of my clothes and climbed onto my stomach. "Let's do this. If I pass out, just roll me over and keep going."

Finn sucked in a hiss. "Oh, sweet heaven and hell, there's a lot of them, Perdi. They're either really scared of you or are just really thorough."

"Scared of me," I answered. "I would be, too."

Carver walked the length of my back and ran his small hands through my matted hair. "There are eighteen back here and one at the base of your skull."

I nodded. "Just do it, please."

"Find a happy place to go to, because we're about to drag you through hell." Carver's first bite ripped my flesh, and it was everything he had promised it would be...hell.

I pushed my face into my hands and growled my pain as the first blistering wave rolled over my body. The second and third bites brought tears to my eyes and the taste of bile to my mouth. The rest of the pain bled together once Finn began to cut. The burn was intense as if my Malice had torn its way through my body, unwilled by me. Like hearing underwater, I heard Finn tell me to roll over, but I couldn't move. I didn't want to, and my limbs didn't either. Slowly, he turned me onto my back, and the pressure of lying on the fresh wounds made me shake. Finn covered my chest and hips with my clothes and left those areas for Carver to inspect. They lifted my arms and checked my armpits. My front didn't have as many, and thankfully there were none in the most delicate areas of my body. I scrunched my face as the pain returned. I didn't scream. There was no room between the pain to do much more than gasp and cry. At the last ward, the world popped around me, and the willingness to rot in the mortal land was gone in an instant. It felt like a weight had lifted off my chest, and I could finally breathe.

"Perdi!" Carver called my name in a panic. "There's something wrong. Your skin is moving."

I jerked from my fade, the happy place I was slowly drifting around in. The urge to pass out was gone. My head was now cleared from the pain and rested somewhere between panic and madness. Carver's frantic yelling caused my heart to pound. Breaking the wards shouldn't have made my skin literally crawl.

"What?" As my mouth opened, I vomited black tar. Carver jumped from my body, and I smiled. "It's okay."

"Perdi." The shadows rolled around me. They felt like a hug from a long-lost friend. The very sight of them clenched my stomach and tightened my throat. My tears, once of pain, were pure liquid joy. "You could not hear us once they marked you with wards. We could not come out, either."

"It's okay, Carver. They're shadows...souls. They belong to Zephyr," Finn called out to the fairy who had ducked behind a stone. "They're with Perdi."

"There are not many of us, we regret," the shadows added.

"I've never been this close to them." Carved slowly inched his way back to me, hesitant. He reached out once, as curious as I had been the first time I had met them, and smiled when the shadows touched his hand in return. "When the shadows returned to Zephyr after you were Taken, he said he couldn't feel the rest. We had thought the worst, but Zephyr said the magick at the Gate could be why he could not feel them or your pearl."

"The shadows made it back?" I asked.

"Yes, a couple of days after you were Taken, they came through the Gate. They told us that you were being held in a Fae trap, being drained of your magick, and were still alive." Carver answered. "The Sluagh tried to come, but the magick held even them back. The wee folk sent all their people in hopes some would be able to help. We sent wave after wave of the smaller Fae, who could still get through the wards. The others, the bigger Fae, couldn't get through."

My stomach flopped, and my heart sped up. "Nix? Where is he? Did he come to Whitwick?"

"He tried. Nix and his people from the Hallows tried. But they were too big and couldn't get through," Carver answered. I didn't want to say out loud that I was happy Nix wasn't here. But Carver knew and patted my hand. "It's okay to be happy Nix is not here. I, too, am happy Orrian did not come."

I pulled my clothes back on and motioned to the shadows. "Can you leave here?"

"No, we can feel the binds that hold all Elphame to these lands. We are weak, as you are, without the magick of Elphame. And to keep them from killing you, we've allowed them to eat our power."

My head dropped. Although I knew the shadows had been bound to Zephyr as a punishment for crimes they had committed so long ago that they didn't remember, I had grown to love them dearly. Leave it to me to love the monsters too wicked to be left alive. But I never looked at them as bound pearls. They had been my friends when I had no one to trust or to love me. And it hurt to know that they had given their lives for me to live. My eyes watered, and my soul felt a little heavier for their sacrifice.

"We smell your sadness, Perdi. We also miss them, but they are now free and have earned that freedom. Zephyr would agree. That you feel grief for their parting means a lot to us. You are the first to love us, and for that, we would give all of who we are to save you."

"Thank you for helping me and keeping me alive...again." I smiled softly. "How many of you came over when we got here?"

"Eighty-three," they answered. "There are twenty-two left. Between releasing some to get home and sacrificing others, we fear we are only a few. If we were not blocked from Elphame, twenty-two would still be a fair number to fight with. But we are limited without our magick."

"Thank you," I whispered. My heart sank. "For your sacrifice."

"Shall we?" Finn asked and pulled off his shirt. "It's not a party unless we're all crying."

"What kind of parties do you go to, where everyone cries?" I laughed.

"No one is free from tears in Elphame, Perdi," he answered.

I looked away as Finn removed the rest of his clothes and positioned himself face down. I hissed the same surprise at how many wards were carved into his body. Carver walked from top to bottom and counted just over a dozen.

"Ready?" I asked.

"No." He lifted his head to face me. "I wasn't even awake for these marks. I slept through them."

"Don't worry, it won't be that bad." I placed my hand on his shoulder and gave him a reassuring squeeze. "Okay, it'll be as bad as you think it will be. But you've had worse cuts than this, I imagine."

"I've never cut myself on purpose. In battle, it's different. I don't feel it. But I've never willingly allowed someone to cut me for any reason."

"Never?" I asked.

"I'm not a witch. There's no reason for me to bleed willingly. Not even in training have I put myself in a situation to be nicked. I'd rather be punched in the face," he answered and shivered from head to toe, like a small wave under his skin. "Bloody hell, I don't like pain."

"Who does?" I asked.

He winked. "There's a kink for everyone."

"Smart ass. Shut up and get ready," I answered. I dragged the tip of my blade over one of the wards.

"Yeah, this does not feel good at all," Finn answered, but he didn't move, flinch or cry out.

"It's not supposed to feel good," I answered and followed Carver down his back and watched as Finn made fists. Carver took one more look before he gave me a thumbs up. We had gotten all the ones on his backside. "Turn over."

Finn rolled onto his back and pulled his shirt over his groin. He breathed deeply, preparing himself for another round of hell. "Okay, I'm ready."

"You have no body hair," I blurted out and felt my face flush.

Finn huffed a small laugh. "Neither does Zephyr, and we all know you've seen him in the buff. We all have. I don't think there's anyone at home who hasn't seen his naked ass."

"I just assumed he didn't like it and removed it," I replied. "Come to think of it, Solas doesn't really have much body hair, either. But Nix is covered in fine hairs, not rough or coarse, almost silky."

"Some Fae don't even have eyelashes, while others are furballs. It depends on their type."

"Type?" I asked. "Aren't all Fae, Fae?"

"No, it's a catchall for us. Sort of like saying all mortals are the same, and you're not," he explained as I cut. "Aos Si are a type of Fae, just as Nix is a gnome and Carver is a fairy. The Aos Si are Aes Sidhe, and most of us have little or no body hair. I think the Gods and Goddesses knew how much it would chaff in our gear."

I nicked the edge of a ward on his lower abdomen. "Thanks for the history lesson."

Finn flinched and scowled. "That is a delicate area, little Crow. Be careful."

I gripped the handle of the blade and closed my eyes. "Please don't call me that, Finn."

He sat straight and grabbed my shoulders. I didn't even know I was crying until he wiped a tear from my cheek. I glanced up and recoiled. It hurt to look him in his eyes, to see the concern for me in the eyes of a Fae. It didn't matter that I was more Fae now than ever before. The memories of my Taking to Elphame were as raw as the day I had landed there. I pulled back and shook my head.

"Perdi, it's okay," Finn whispered.

"Just… Finn, please, let's finish this," I answered. "Please. I can't break down here. If I do, I don't know if I'll stop. I don't want to die or be the cause of anyone else's death because I'm sad and wounded. I'd rather die for better reasons."

He lay back, and I followed Carver as he pointed out the smaller symbols. I was careful, but my hands still shook. His front had as many as his backside, but at least they'd left his groin area untouched. My hand wasn't steady enough to be slicing up flesh in places he'd prefer I wasn't holding a knife against on a good day.

I held Finn's shirt off his groin while Carver took one last look and nodded. "Finn, did you know your birthmark is on your...?" Carver poked his head out from under the shirt.

"And I don't need to know that." I dropped the shirt onto Carver and moved away from Finn. I needed a few feet of space between us before I lost grip on my carefully won control. Finn dressed without asking questions, but I felt the weight of his stare.

"What do we do now?" Carver asked.

"I think I can do a spell, just enough to let the shadows through the wards. I doubt I can do much more than that," I answered.

"Perdi." Carver tapped my leg. "The wards... They are greater than what was on your body. Those who have attempted to so much as touch them have all died. I fear, if you attempt it, you will perish."

"Carver is right," Finn added. "We can come here, but we can't ever leave. Just nearing the border feels like you're burning off the outer layers of your skin. I've circled this plot of land many times, and there is nowhere that won't cook off your soul. And Zephyr isn't here to help you. If you die, you're as dead as the rest of us."

"We're going to die here anyway. It might as well be for an attempted escape," I answered. "We'll need to find the others. We'll have to remove their wards before we do anything else. They'll only grow weaker because of the symbols."

"We don't think an escape will work." The shadows rolled around me like a hug. "While you were unconscious, we could hear what was happening. The mortal realm is waging war against Elphame. Every witch has come to the aid of Whitwick. Together, with the magick spooled from your souls, they plan to curse the Fae and seal them inside Elphame. Any Fae who have come through the Gate have either died or will be put here to die. The wards that keep us all here, on these cursed lands, are designed to kill any who attempt to leave or meddle with the wall around us. It is dark magick and curses those who try."

"Then we haven't much time to stand around. The sooner we act, the better. The longer we stay here, the weaker we will become," I answered. "Carver, Finn, do you know where the others are?"

"Yes. Up higher. We keep as far away from the border as we can," Carver answered.

I nodded. "We rest tonight, and at first light, we head up."

"We'll go grab our gear," Finn answered. "Be back shortly."

I nodded and tucked myself into the corner of the room. I told the shadows to keep guard at the mouth of the cave. I curled into a ball and fought against the exhaustion that worked to drag me under. The moment my eyes were closed, I dreamed. I watched my Taking. I could feel the lashes from my first night at the Golden Court. Flashes of memory played over and over, twisting my mind into a ball of doubt and fear. I could hear the music that played in the background of each ball, barely covering the screams that were cut short by death and laughter. A woman dragged herself through the crowd and clawed at my ankles, begging me to help her. Me vomiting on her shoes and humiliating her in her final moments stabbed my heart like a knife. If nothing else, Elphame had taught me how cruel we each could be to save our own skin. I wondered how many others laughed simply because they were too scared to die in her place. One act of kindness, helping her, and I would have been killed for it. The mask I had worn would have fallen off, and all the monstrous things I had done would have been for nothing. Until now, I hadn't understood how costly kindness could be and why so few spent it frivolously.

Chapter Six

I woke up to Finn settling in beside me. Carver was tucked into a small bag on Finn's lap. As scared as I was, I was thankful to be woken from my dream. At least awake, I had the power to act on my fears, even if all I could do was run away. Asleep, I was paralyzed, and nothing I could do would change my path. I couldn't hide from my dreams.

"Nightmares?" Finn asked. "I've been having them, too."

I pulled myself sitting and put the distance back between us. "I don't know what's real and what's a figment of my fear."

"Tell me about your dream. I'll tell you if it happened," Finn replied.

I shook my head. "You weren't there for my Taking. How could you know?"

"You're reliving your Taking?" he asked and hissed. "Nothing like having the biggest and most terrifying moment of your life replaying over and over. I'm dreaming of wars I've won, but in my dreams, I lose."

"It feels more horrible than when I lived it."

"It always does. When you're in the actual moment, your focus is on your survival. It's only after that you notice smells or sounds or faces or wounds you don't remember even getting, all of which end up haunting you more than the event itself. It's those small things that sting the most. That's what I'm dreaming of…those I couldn't save. But what I'm dreaming didn't happen as I know it did."

"There are too many versions in my mind. I don't know which one is real. Some play out as I originally remember, but with added details like laughter or my name called or how the fog moves against the ground. Other times, I dream Solas dragged me out of my house by my hair. I dream of being tortured at the Golden Court. I dream of being forced into the bedchamber of King Aelfdene while Solas watched and wouldn't help me."

"I can't comment on what happened in Whitwick during your Taking, but we were there, on the Elphame side," he answered. "You weren't dragged in by your hair. You came through willingly and on your own two feet. But you did pass out once you stepped out of the Gate onto Elphame soil. Solas carried you while you were puking and mumbling curses at him. He dropped you on the ground twice before getting you to the boat. Nix was livid, screaming at Solas. Nix has never backed down from anyone when it has come to you, not even against the nightmare of Elphame."

"I don't remember being dropped, and I don't remember seeing you."

"You rarely see Aos Si unless we want you to," he replied. "We weren't allowed to interfere because of the oath. And because Zephyr was locked in the Golden Court dungeon, all we could do was watch," he replied. "I don't know what happened at the Golden Court day to day. The eyes and ears we had in there didn't report on such things. But if it helps, I don't believe Solas would have watched Aelfdene force himself onto you. And truly, if he had, I doubt you'd have remained with him."

"He didn't stop it from happening to other women," I countered.

"Neither did you," Finn replied, and I jerked at his comment. "It is always easiest to point out the failings of others but never our own. You are foolish if you have this grand notion in your mind that he should have saved everyone. He picked the hill to die on, and that hill was you. It's the same hill everyone else chose," he answered. "If you couldn't save them, why would you think anyone else could? The world doesn't work that way. Just because you are now looking back on it and feeling guilty doesn't mean it could have been different."

"If Zephyr was locked away, why didn't any of you try to rescue him?" I asked.

"He forbade any interfering with his master plan of saving a Crow. He went there to help you. If we'd have rescued him, how would he rescue you? If Solas had stopped the suffering of others, how could he stop yours?" he asked. "We wanted to help, but we couldn't. We'd have risked more lives with our actions than we'd have saved—just like Solas would have, had he saved those you regret not saving."

"Everyone's life is worth saving," I countered.

He huffed a small laugh. "It's lovely to think that, in your little world of right and wrong and fairness. But in the real world, where the rest of us live and die, there is no room for such pretty things. Nothing is fair. Nothing will ever be, and no amount of regret or wishing will make it so. Had we tried to help Zephyr or you or those marched to their deaths for entertainment, we'd have broken an oath, started a war and sentenced the mortal world to the suffering of becoming a Crow. Have you enjoyed your Crow wings so much to wish them upon other innocents?"

"No," I answered and groaned.

"Neither would I. Although sitting here now, I wouldn't regret a few mortals losing their hide to Elphame," he answered, and a part of me agreed. I wouldn't lose sleep if the witches ended up as Crows. "Fear has a way of kicking us when we're down, making us wish for things we shouldn't want. It makes us double back in our mind and look for ways to have changed the fate we sit in."

I nodded. "It's hard to know what's real and what's not. What do I really fear, and what was I made to fear? I feel like I know what the truth is, but it gets confusing in my head. My soul and brain are in conflict."

"If you get stuck, ask yourself if Solas would have allowed it? If Zephyr would allow that to happen to you? And would either have hidden it from you? Truly, would Nix hide it from you or allow a single one of them to have harmed you and not faced his wrath? Of all those you surround yourself with, one of them would have told you the truth by now."

"I dream that Zephyr was there, watching. Even though I know it's not possible, he was locked away, the memories are still there. I dream Nix invited them into my home and watched as they dragged me away."

"Nix would die before he willingly allowed someone to harm you. I imagine he did what he could with the little chance he had. He didn't watch. He followed you into Elphame, back to the wars and games and pain. He helped you the best he could and suffered for you when he could," Finn replied. "But, unfortunately, memories don't have to be real to hurt us. They simply need to be there for us to feel their sting."

I sighed. "The witches have taken everything and warped it into something much more awful than it already was."

"They've given you doubt and fear, a deadly combination to be plagued with. If I were on the other side of the battlefield from you, I'd know I had won before even lifting my sword. They were hoping you'd become the tool they needed to win a war against an army that would never kill you. But I don't think they counted on how strong you are, that you'd never become a tool if what they asked of you was not the right thing to do. So, they played to your fear when they couldn't overcome your morals. Imagine if it had worked and you stood against Elphame? We'd lose simply because we would hesitate to kill you."

"I doubt that, Finn. It would hurt Solas, but he would kill me to save his people."

"No, I don't think he would, or you'd already be dead," he answered. "He became the Taker of Crows to save you. He waged war over and over to save you. And if he somehow changed his mind, do you think Zephyr would allow it? You're the only other like him. He's probably chewing his way through the Gate to get to you. You are his only family, Perdi. We're all family, but you are his very bloodline. He'd kill us all for you. If you think for a minute that Zephyr wouldn't have to get in line behind Solas to save you, you don't pay attention. And, if some strange twist of fate occurred and neither of them fought for you, do you think Nix would stand by? Nix, who is owed countless favors and oaths, would save you on his own. Even I owe the wee gnome. He auctions off apple pies for favors. Most of the Aos Si owe him." He inched closer and tried to hide it under the guise of getting comfortable. "When we get out of here—and we will, when the Gate opens back up—who do you think will come through first? It will be the Aos Si. They will storm Whitwick because you're our family." Finn closed the distance between us, and I didn't pull away. "Although you're being tormented right now, you know in your heart that on the other side of that Gate is a world of people who love you and will come for you every time...because that's what family does. We wage war for each other. We go into hell, blind, for each other."

"What I would give for this to end."

"For what to end?" he asked. "There happens to be a lot on the table for you to clear off."

"The Gate. My entire life is that bloody Gate. All it's ever brought is suffering. I tried to close it and failed. Then Solene destroyed it, looking for the very Fae that took her life, and it sentenced the Satyr to be hunted. And now, because of that cursed thing, we're stuck in this hellhole."

"This was coming, Perdi, long before you stepped through the Gate. Your story was written by Fate long ago," Finn replied. "Unfortunately, you can't skip chapters in your life. You were born to come here, just as much as I was born to be here with you. If you could skip to the end, you'd learn nothing, and you'd miss the parts that are worth every ounce of pain. But if I ever find a way to take this burden of the Gate from you, I will."

"As poetic as that is, Finn, I'm so fucking over it. I'm over the lessons. I'm over having life scratch away at my soul. I'm over the games, the wars and losses so great that my soul tastes blood."

"You're not over it, or you'd be dead. You'd have killed yourself or simply allowed someone else to do it. Stop trying to be more than what you are. It's okay to be scared. Being brave has nothing to do with how scared you are. You're emotionally tired, and that's an acceptable place to be right now."

"It's uncomfortable."

He laughed. "All of life is uncomfortable—all of it, not just the bad parts. Growth, in any direction, good or bad, is painful and scary. You've never been here before, this moment in time. You don't know the person you are today. This version of yourself, here in the cave, you've never met her. It is uncomfortable to meet a version of yourself that you never thought you'd become. But come tomorrow, you'll have grown used to who you are today. Give yourself a little time, breathe through it and know that today will be both your hardest and your least difficult day when looking back."

"How reassuring." I groaned at the thought that I'd consider this to be easier than what was left to come.

"It wasn't meant to be. It's simply just the truth. I've lived many lifetimes, Perdi, and today is not the worst day I've lived, but it's also not my best day. Knowing that I've been in worse situations, seen more horror than Whitwick could possibly muster and knowing that I've done a hell of a lot worse to get home than what I'll do here makes this a lot less scary for me. And I think you're afraid not of where you are but of what you know you'll do to leave this place. Facing yourself will be scarier than anything else we'll do in the coming days. Take it from someone who has tried to outrun himself for decades, who you are will always win the race," he said, and I smiled a little at his pep talk. He was much smoother than Zephyr was, but Zephyr has lived for centuries. Time tended to wear words into sharp sticks. "It helps to know that although today is hard, I'll never have to do today again. I'll never have to see this day again. I'll never feel exactly like this again. Tomorrow may be worse, but today will help me ease into it. And if tomorrow is better, then the sacrifice of today is all the more worth it."

"I understand what you're saying, but I still want it to end. Just skip to the end and let this all be over," I mumbled. "I don't want to kill just to live. That's not living."

"We all want our suffering to end. But the only way to get to the end is by going through the middle, however painful that will be," he answered. "Get some rest. I'll wake you up if you're dreaming."

"I'd never get any sleep if you woke me up every time I had a bad dream," I countered. I leaned into the wall and got comfortable as the shadows settled over the three of us.

"I've never been inside the shadows like this. I've only ever been moved around by them, not settled inside. This feels tight and uncomfortable. I can taste tears in here. Sweet mercy, what kind of tortured souls have you guys been dragging around?" Finn whispered. "I don't know how you can stand it. It's fucking awful. God, it's like I'm swimming in an ocean of sadness. Can't you feel that?"

"That's not the shadows, Finn," I answered. "You're feeling me. They amplify the emotions of those within. If I was still bound to them, we'd be feeling their emotions as well. Since I'm not, you're only feeling me. I'm sorry I can't control it like Zephyr did."

"It feels like standing inside my head during my first war — sad, scared and horrified with myself and what I saw. It's like walking through a battlefield and being the only survivor."

"I can feel you, too," I replied, then squirmed at my sudden discomfort. I could feel Finn's body, his pulse fluttering against my skin, every breath he took and released. "Finn, how hard have you ever been punched?"

"I was once hit in the chest hard enough for my heart to stop," he answered. "Why?"

"If you even touch me, I'll make sure your new measurement of pain includes being hit by me." I pulled myself away from him. "You may feel my dread in here, but I also can sense your emotions. You feel needy for…please tell me you're not thinking of sex."

"It isn't sex I'm thinking of," he answered and laughed. "Calm down. You don't do it for me. You're very much not my type, no offense. I'm down for some risky stuff, but dying for it isn't my idea of a good time. I don't know who would kill me first, Zephyr or Solas."

"It would be me," I answered.

"I was just thinking of home…not of bedding you."

"Do you have a partner at home?" I asked. "Is that why you're a little happier at the moment?"

"No." He laughed again. The current within the shadows shifted with his amusement. "My life is difficult to invite others into for anything longer than a night or two. I am Aos Si. It isn't an easy path to walk — and harder for those not made for digging graves. One day I might not come home, and that's a big ask of someone to live with each time I leave. The reaction you've so eloquently pointed out is the same energy most give off when thinking of sex, but for me, it has nothing to do with it. Rest assured, Perdi, I'm not thinking of that. I'm thinking of what we'll have to do to get home. And the prospects of war tend to cross the signals in my brain, and my body reacts to the threat, the promise, the battle. For someone like me, the possibility of unleashing all I am is exciting. I've never released all of my awful abilities, but the thought of it does a lot to my body."

"You're made for more than war, Finn." I moved from the wall and closed the distance between us. I leaned my head against his arm. "You're made for greatness."

"As are you, little...Perdi." He stopped himself from saying what he likely thought might drive me away.

"One day," I answered.

"One day," he repeated. He lifted his arm and pulled me into him. I was stiff at first, then finally settled into his warmth. "We'll get home, or we'll die trying. It's as simple as it is difficult."

"Have you ever been cut off from Elphame before?"

"Not in this way, no. But all Aos Si have been dumped in the middle of nowhere, ironed and have had to make their way back. Zephyr does it to us all the time. Grabs us while we're asleep, dead tired from training or war, and picks some random spot and drops us there. Once, I had just stepped off the battlefield after hours of fighting in a full-out war. The moment I was done cleaning myself up and climbed into bed, he snagged me as I drifted off to sleep."

"Does he give you clothes? Because he never gives me clothes." I laughed.

"No. If you were naked when Zephyr found you, that's how he takes you. I've had to hike the entire Winter Court, completely nude, before I learned to sleep in full leathers," he replied. "I used to curse his name every time, but I knew he was watching, and I never gave up. I think I kept going just to spite him."

"I don't think I would have lived through training," I replied.

"But you have. Zephyr trains you every day, just in different ways. You're not Aos Si. You're Finis, so your lessons will be different from ours. We've watched him with you. He's no easier on you than he is on any of us. We have all come to watch you and Zephyr fistfight — hours of hand-to-hand, him chasing you, you chasing him. You never give up until you're out cold, and even then, you come back swinging. Sure, he wins in the end, but you've made him pay for it every time." Finn's laugh was touchable in the shadows. I could feel it glide across my skin. "If he dumped you in the middle of nowhere, I have no doubt you'd find your way home."

"I'd stop and ask for help," I countered.

"That's the point he made with me, Perdi. He teaches you to count on yourself, but he also teaches you to use the tools around you, the ones that'll help you win," he replied. "He stopped dumping me in the middle of nowhere once I learned the lessons I fought against. I had made it from the Hallows, barely, to the Winter Court. It was the dead of winter, I had fallen off a cliff, and been chased by leprechauns before I'd made it to Winter Court territory, completely nude, ironed and freezing parts of my body I've grown to love fondly. I finally requested passage through Faolan's lands. Faolan gave me clothes, food and drink and helped me across his territory. For me, the lesson was that I could ask for help when I needed it, that not everyone was my enemy. Before then, I'd never asked, and I always paid for it. All my training was for that lesson. I've always been a great fighter and topped almost every class. But fighting was never my problem. Peace was. Learning that I'm not always at war was a painful lesson."

"What the hell is he trying to teach me? It feels like all he does is beat the crap out of me."

"He is teaching you how to survive, how to get back up, how to not live in your wounds, how to think through the pain. Your other lessons will come. For now, he's teaching you how to live without him. It's the same thing he teaches all of us at the beginning, that he won't always be there to help. Take this moment… He is not here to save you. But he's taught you everything you need to know to save yourself. If I weren't here, you'd still survive because he has taught you how to live, not just exist. You knew to get out of the open, collect resources, assess your damage, then find a way back home. Most would have lost their cool and died…but you didn't."

"That sounds like Zeph," I replied.

"And Solas… He has guided you to listen to your soul above all else. Where Zephyr teaches you peace, Solas has taught you to war if peace fails. It is through the peace you will know how to calm yourself, how to ground yourself and how to see beyond your fear. And through war, you learn not to back down, not to give up, to survive when the cards are stacked against you." Finn hugged me tighter. "And now, Perdi, you see that your memories may not be as accurate as you remember them. Zephyr is many things, but he is not the monster you remember. And Solas? Well, he is the monster we all know he is, but *for* you, not against you. He eats your monsters. He always has and always will, until his last breath. Many things were done, but Solas has always lived and breathed for your very life. You are his sun and moon, and because of you, he is a better man, a better friend and a better king. He's someone the rest of us are willing to follow — not because of titles, but because he has earned it."

"Thanks, Finn. Although my memories are nasty as hell, hearing your stories somehow helps settle my soul."

"Now, I'm thinking about sex. Shall we discuss that in as much detail? I'm chock full of those stories, as well. Allow me to regale you with a story of my first time with a water nymph. It really was a night of many firsts..."

"Good night, Finn."

"Good night, little Crow," he replied.

"Don't call me that," I muttered.

"As you wish, little Crow."

Chapter Seven

Finn woke me up throughout the night. Twice, I had tried to run, and once, he held me down and covered my mouth to keep me from screaming. By morning, I woke to him wrapped around me, holding me in the cave. The shadows kept us covered and warm while Finn and Carver took turns staying awake and keeping a watching eye for those who didn't fare as well as we had. Some Fae who had come to the cursed lands, cut off from Elphame, were feral and had to be 'put down', as they called it. Even as they said the words, I saw how badly it hurt them to kill their own people to save themselves and the other survivors. Without a doubt, before this was over, I'd feel that same pain, but my reason would have nothing to do with being humane.

I followed Finn and Carver out of the rock cave and hiked behind them up the hill, sticking close to the tree line and out of sight. Having the wards cut from my body had helped me recover enough to not struggle for each breath. I wasn't at full strength, but I wasn't shambling about, tripping on air. Each wound hurt as badly as it had the day before, my arms still burned, but my heart no longer felt sluggish and fading. Food, water and rest had made a difference, although I still felt exhausted, hungry and thirsty.

"How the hell did a month pass?" I asked.

The shadows crawled along the ground at my side. "We kept you asleep."

"Why?" I asked. "Maybe I could have stopped this."

"You would have died had we not," they answered. "Imagine if you had been awake like the others were. You'd have died from the pain of it all. Or worse, you'd have lived through it and remembered what they did to your body. Perdi, your soul still hasn't healed from the island. To be brutally honest, you haven't fully healed from your first Taking. How you're up and walking is beyond us. Your soul is tattered and broken from too many trials. We kept you asleep so as to not damage it any more than it already is. A Crow with broken wings cannot survive wicked things."

Carver slowed his pace and walked beside me. His little body was still just as graceful without his wings. "Be grateful you were not aware, Perdi. I was...most of us were. The majority of us didn't live through it. It felt like my life was being pulled from me, and my soul was being burned alive. I thought I was dying, and when I realized I hadn't, I truly wanted it. When they took my wings...it was horrible. I asked for death but was put here instead. Had I slept through it, I'd have been thankful."

"I'm so sorry, Carver." I wanted to tell him I wished he hadn't come but didn't know how to say that I merely wished he hadn't suffered. I didn't want to take away his loyalty and honor by wishing out loud. "If I was awake, maybe I could have helped? Maybe I could have come up with a plan sooner. Instead, I was asleep, causing all this."

"You didn't do this," Carver answered. His voice was stern. "You tried to help the mortals. And when you couldn't do the impossible, it wasn't you who called the witches into Whitwick. You didn't ask them to do any of this. And you didn't take my wings, nor do I blame you. You would have died for nothing, like so many others. Do not *ever* blame yourself for this. You carry none."

The shadows rolled up my legs as if they were trying to hug me. "To go home, you'll do worse things. There will be enough blame to go around for what's yet to come. Don't add what the mortals have done to the reasons you'll hurt later."

"You said I'd regret not coming back when we were on the island," I said to the shadows. "You told me something was off here, and I said to let them suffer. I should have paid closer attention to what was happening here. Maybe this wouldn't be happening if I had done my duty."

"You did your duty, just as we did ours. We did not know this was going to happen. We thought, at most, the mortals would be foolish enough to go to war with Elphame…but not this, Perdi. We would have told you of this. We would have told Zephyr and Solas. But we didn't think their creativity would include what has happened to you and our people."

"They did war, in the only way they knew how to fight against the Fae. It's the same way I fight…with magick. I cannot win unless I use my Malice," I answered. "I regret not paying closer attention to the Gate."

"And now it is their turn to regret," Finn added. "I understand that these are your people, Perdi, but what they have done, they will pay for. Whether we collect their payment for this or Elphame does, no one will allow this debt to stand."

"They aren't my people...not anymore," I answered. "And yes, they will pay."

Carver climbed up the side of Finn and stood on his shoulder while I followed behind. It reminded me of how Nix rode on my shoulders, and a sudden wave of homesickness washed over me. As glad as I was to not have Nix on my shoulder while we walked through enemy lands, I missed him horribly. There weren't many times I had been in Whitwick, since early childhood, without Nix close by.

"You smell of wishes and sadness." The shadows called my attention out of my dread.

"I miss home," I answered.

"As do we. It is unsettling to be cut off from Elphame. This is a first for us. Although we dislike the feeling, we do not regret coming with you."

"I'm glad you're with me but sorry for the reason," I replied.

"As are we," they replied. "We will scout ahead," the shadows said and rolled in and out of the trees, under every rock and into every dip.

They were my eyes and ears, as always. Being in the mortal realm didn't change who we were. If anything, being away from home only amplified our vigilance. Up ahead, as Finn and Carver joked, both of them were on high alert, scanning every inch around us. You can take the soldier out of Elphame, but they were still a soldier, wherever they landed.

The walk in the hills reminded me of hiking as a child. From the smells unhindered by magick to the sounds I couldn't hear in Elphame, it was exactly how I remembered it. They were the only memories I had that weren't tarnished and twisted by the witches. They were the only ones where I wasn't forced into a life that hurt. Before the Gate, before my Taking, life had been simple. I had hopes and dreams, and none of them were Fae. None of them were war or death or the wonder of how I'd make it another day. The fear was always there, floating under the surface, but it was far enough away that I still planned on growing old in Whitwick. But once I was Taken, my dreams soured, and now I dreamed of death and war and anything I could do to survive. And I didn't know who I blamed more for that—mortals who perverted my memories or Fae who had given me the memories to begin with.

"We're here," Carver announced and pulled my mind from a future I'd never have in a place that tried to take the very life I ended up with. "Wait here. I'll tell the others."

I waited outside of a den carved out of the mountain. It reminded me of hiding with Nix inside an Elphame fox den and being worried the beast would come home to give birth, eating us in the process. Carver went in to warn the others that he had brought another back with him. I stared down the mountain and could feel the night crawling in, casting shadows over the land as dusk strolled by. What had been beautiful in the daylight was subtly ominous with the pressing of the night. Carver poked his head out and waved me in. Once he was sure the others wouldn't scatter, I went in with the shadows. A small fire sat at the rear of the den. Small stones and logs circled it. Carver went around the group, all of whom were Unseelie, most from the Dark Court, with a few of Faolan's people. They all were as surprised as Carver had been that I was still alive. I knelt and thanked each one for coming, hugged some and held others in my hands that were too small to hug.

We spent the rest of what was left of the evening carving the wards from tiny bodies. Most of them didn't flinch, and it broke my heart. Those who did, it enraged me to see them so broken, to have suffered for no other reason than being Fae. It was an odd feeling, because not that long ago, I suffered for no other reason than being mortal. But those who I knelt before hadn't hurt the mortals or me. The wee folk never came to Whitwick for the Taking. They hadn't hunted humans for any reason. For some, this hellish trip had been their first time away from Elphame. And as angry as I still was that any mortal had become a Crow, I didn't believe all Fae should suffer for it. The person responsible was dead, and that was enough for me.

Finn and I fed blood to the Fairies and fruit to the others while Carver told them of our plans. We would see if there was a way out, and if not, we'd send the shadows for help. Although most appeared not to believe we stood a chance, no one spoke out about it. They were willing to try. Worse case, they'd die, which was much more appealing than the already likely ending, should we do nothing at all. No one wanted to die a coward in the back of a den.

"When do we try?" Carver asked. "First light?"

"Now," I answered. "We can stay hidden at night. We'll stand out like a sore thumb in broad daylight. They'll feel what I do to the wards, and I'd rather not be standing around in the afternoon sun for them to pick us off with ease. If they're going to hunt us, let's make it a little harder for them to kill us."

"Let's go to the wall of wards," Finn announced. "It isn't far from here."

The others packed up the little bits of food they had and were ready before I had even stood. They were skittish, nervous of what the night held in a land that had only given them pain. The mortal world was not their own and was as unfamiliar to them as Elphame had been to me. I remember my first night on the run and exactly how it felt as we left the illusion of safety the cave gave us. With Carver in the lead, we followed him through the darkness. My shadows pointed out roots and other things I'd trip on and lower limbs where I'd have brained myself. The creatures moved with ease as if night were the only time they came out. I remembered what it was like to be the prey, the smallest and weakest in a world of what I once thought were giants. Carver stopped and pointed at the wall that locked us inside. I could feel the magick in the air. It prickled along my skin and filled my hair with static. The moon and stars shimmered a reflection that rolled across a glass dome, covering us like animals in a cage. The wall was streaked in magick, familiar and different at once.

"It's my magick," I told them all. "It's been sealed with my blood but mixed with magick not of my own. It feels like me, but there's something else there. My guess would be the witches who came to Whitwick are the ones who lent a hand in the creation of this spelled wall."

"What does that mean? Can you break the spell?" Finn asked.

"There are only two ways to break a witch's spell, their death or someone much more powerful," I answered. "I am not more powerful than I was when this was cast. If anything, I'm weaker today. And I don't plan on dying any time soon for it to break. Though, if I die, all of you should run fast and far before they bring it back up."

"Is it more powerful than the spell at the island?" Finn asked.

"No, but when we broke the spells that hid the island, I had a small army to pull power from. We don't have that here," I answered.

"Can we help?" Carver asked. "There are many souls here that you can eat."

I shook my head. "Even if I wanted to—which I don't—I couldn't. Elphame magick is cut off here. I'm too close to a mortal now, as are the rest of you. I can't even feel my Malice, let alone use her to eat your souls. Without Elphame magick, I'm a witch, and witches don't eat souls like the Finis do."

"Can you still spell?" Finn asked.

"We're going to find out," I replied. "It won't be on any grand scale, though."

"Perdi"—the shadows rose up by my side—"if we leave and payment comes, you will not survive it. You are too weak to pay."

"But you will be free, and you can bring aid back to the others."

"If you can't get out, how will others get in?" they asked.

"When you can, find Solas and tell him what has happened," I answered. "He'll find a way. He's mighty convincing when he's pissed off."

"No, we don't think that will work. If the Gate is sealed, we won't be able to get to Elphame or back in here with you. You will be stuck here, without us, waiting for a rescue that won't be coming. But, if you can make a hole, we all can leave now, together." The shadows moved in front of me. It was a nervous movement of theirs. "They will feel what you've done, and they'll kill you all if you stay here."

Finn tapped my shoulder. "Mortals have come before when they've felt Fae meddling with the wards, and they've slaughtered all they could find. If we do this, the hole must be big enough for all of us to leave, or we all will die, including you."

The shadows twisted in agreement. "Once we're out of here, perhaps we can draw enough power to get us away. It may not be far, but it may be enough. Then we can go for help."

"I don't have the power for that. I want to, I'm willing to try, but I don't have the energy," I answered and lifted my disfigured arms. "I've been drained of everything—blood, power, magick."

"Use us," they replied. "We are pure Elphame. Take half of us. You don't need your Malice to use us if we give ourselves willingly. You may be drained of Elphame, but you are still Fae."

I shook my head, saddened they'd suggest such a thing. "But that would kill you. It would destroy those I used."

"It certainly would," they answered. "The silver lining is, those you consumed would be free. We both win. Those you take will have earned their freedom, and you will be granted yours."

I knelt and released a long and frustrated breath. "There are never easy choices anymore. It doesn't matter if I stand in the mortal world or the Fae. Every choice feels like life and death."

Finn crouched beside me. "Every choice *is* life and death, even the ones that are simple and easy. Every choice we make creates a path to life or death. It may not even be our own that we unknowingly decide on. You have choices here, Perdi, and I don't envy you for them. But you must decide. You know we can't stay here. We will all die in here. Out there, at least, you give everyone a chance, including yourself."

"I know," I agreed. "But knowing doesn't make it feel any better."

"It never will. Trust me," Finn replied.

"When I do the spell, you'll all need to be quick," I spoke to the others.

"You all must stand close together. The wee ones should link arms so we don't leave anyone behind when we pull everyone across," the shadows said, and the wee folk gripped each other's hands.

I stood and finally nodded in agreement. "Let's find the weakest point in the wall. It'll take less energy. Less of you will need to die."

"Perdi, we're already dead. You see this as some sort of sacrifice. We see this as freedom," the shadows answered. "Do not feel sadness."

"Perhaps I'll just miss you."

"And those of us who leave will miss you."

In complete silence, we walked the warded wall, focusing on dips, rocks, fallen trees...anything that would cause a hiccup in the magick. I stopped at a cluster of rocks. The spell struggled to grab onto every angle and jutting stone. This was it. This was our chance, and I was filled with grief and doubt. If it didn't work, we'd be dead come sunrise. And if it did, I'd eat half of the shadows, and we could still end up dead.

"When this is done, when we're out, everyone needs to get away from me. The witches will be looking for me, specifically. You'll all have a better chance at survival if you're not with me. As soon as you can, get to the Gate, and go home if you can. If you can't, hide and remain out of sight until the Gate is open again. If you find any other Fae, tell them what happened and hide them, too. It doesn't matter what court they're from. Help all the Fae you find."

Carver nodded. "Good luck, Perdi."

I knelt down and pulled a few hairs from my head. I used the knife from my bag and dragged it across my hand. With my adrenaline soaring, the wound only stung for a few seconds. I felt the shadows who would be sacrificed rest on my shoulders. With a shaking voice and tears in my eyes, I whispered my spell and pressed my bloody hands into the earth. The shadows uncurled, and I drank down their power.

With knot one, my spell has begun.
With knot two, my heart is true.
With knot three, so mote it be.
With knot four, this spell can hold us no more.
With knot five, we offer a sacrifice.
With knot six, this freedom spell is fixed.
With knot seven, the holding spell will lessen.
With knot eight, this spell is our fate.
With knot nine, the cost is not just mine.
So mote it be.

The spell shuddered against the rocks it had barely held on to. It was enough for the shadows to drag us from the cursed lands. We were yanked as far as the remaining shadows could carry us. When we landed, tucked into another den, half of the shadows left for Elphame, the rest tucked around me and hid me from the world. Carver and the others bolted. As payment came hard and fast, my last thought was that those who had come to Whitwick to find me now had a chance, and the shadows who had cared for me were now free. Whatever came next, I had done what I could for those who had done all they could for me—and that was enough of a win for me.

Chapter Eight

"Why didn't you leave?" I asked before I opened my eyes. I could hear him moving in and out of the den I was tucked into.

"I came here to find you. We all did. And we all leave together or not at all." Finn pushed a piece of bark toward me, mounded with small berries and roots. "I refilled your canteen with fresh water."

"You all stayed?" I asked.

"I am with you. The others have gone toward Whitwick, hoping to draw them away from you."

"That's not what I wanted." I groaned out my frustration and worry.

"Lucky for us, you are not the queen of the mortal realm." He grinned. "And I doubt very much you'll string us up by our necks for treason when we get home."

"You, perhaps, but not the others." I smiled.

"You'll have to fight Zephyr for the honors," he replied. "Be grateful I stayed, Perdi. I tracked four guards from Whitwick when they came to inspect what we had done to the wards."

"Did you bury them or leave them splayed as a warning?" I asked.

He grinned. "I dumped them over a hill into a pond. It'll take a good week before they bob to the surface."

"Thank you, Finn," I finally replied. I was grateful to not be alone but sad that I made him a bigger target for the witches.

"Always, Perdi," he replied. "Do you feel Elphame yet?"

"No, not really," I answered. "It's a trickle, maybe less. You?"

"Barely, but it's enough for me. I do not depend on it as much as most Fae."

"The Aos Si do not use magick, ever?"

"Not in the way others do. We use it, but we do not depend on it or need it all that often. When we train, Zephyr hangs iron around our necks to dull the magick. It teaches us to reach beyond our Fae abilities, to depend on ourselves before anything else. He forces us to become who we are meant to be and not who others think we are. It's an advantage for us. You've seen our wars. Armies deplete themselves of magick and fall because of it, and we do not buckle, because we are not using magick at all."

"Sounds like a painful lesson to learn," I answered.

"It is not comfortable at first, but you get used to it."

"What is your power, your Fae magick?" I asked. "Solas is a bloody nightmare, Zephyr eats souls, Faolan is a winter storm that kills everything it touches like frost on a vine. Everyone seems to have a nifty trick. What's yours?"

"You see the worst in people, little Crow," he said, and I cringed at the name. He raised his eyebrows and smiled. "You're choosing to see the parts that terrify you. Zephyr eats souls, but he can also heal them, find them from across worlds, can give life to others. Solas is a nightmare, but he eats the nightmares in others and can eat more fear than Faolan's Bodach. He replaces that fear with courage and determination. And Faolan? Although I don't know him well, I can feel the calm he sends into the world. His very presence makes you think of memories worth having. You? You can eat a room of souls in one gulp, but you're the first person to stand in front of them and wage war to save them. You will cook your own soul to charcoal to save one innocent who likely wasn't worth the pain. But to you, every life matters. For every horror you see in others, there is another side to them if you look hard enough."

"But you've never really scared me. Of all the Aos Si I've met, fear is not how I would describe you," I answered. "You've made my Malice uncomfortable, but I haven't feared you as I've feared so many others."

"And that, little Crow, is my power. My mother was a Seer, and my father was an Aos Si. I can see what you desire and want and twist it for whatever gain I choose. I can both mentally and physically overpower just about anyone. But more than that, you will trust me as I take your life, and you will want every horrible moment of it—and that's not even with me touching you. You will open your door, invite me in and strap yourself down for me. You will beg for more as I peel the skin from your meat. The worst part is that I can make you believe you want more or take my magick away, where you suddenly realize what is happening, and you then suffer horribly, powerless, while I do as I wish. I know your worst fears and can warp them into a reality that is so much worse. I can stand yards away, and you'll tear your own flesh from your bones while I tinker around in your head."

"That's a terrifying thought," I answered.

"It should be, and that's not even the worst of who I can become. If I touch you, it can be so much worse."

"How much worse could it get?"

"Much worse. Think…attract the notice of the Gods. Imagine living decades in your worst nightmare while only seconds have passed." His body shuddered. "If you want my secrets, I want yours. Tell me the why behind wanting to know first."

I struggled to explain in a way that didn't sound silly, rolling my reasons around in my mind until I gave up and went with whatever version made even the remotest amount of sense. "It sounds foolish to say it out loud, but I guess I just wanted to know if I was the only one fated to share my suffering with others, that someone out there was a bigger monster than me. Zeph never talks about the darkest parts of his power, but I feel it. Whenever I open that door to my abilities, it doesn't want to close. And I don't just want to leave the door open. I want to fill the room with shadows — and not just the souls of people who deserve to die. I want to take them all. My Malice is starving all the bloody time. But that's not the worst of my power. I'm not just Finis. I'm a witch."

"Rest assured, there are worse things out there than a little Crow. But I pose the same question to you. How much worse could it get than stealing the souls of those you kill? If allowed to roam unchecked, that is a terribly rare and utterly destructive power, but it's not the worst one I've seen."

"Finn, they don't have to be dead for me to take their pearls. On the island, I took their souls before they died. In that instant, between deciding if they live or die, I could have forced them to fight for us, to kill their own people, but chose their deaths instead. But it doesn't matter if they are dead or alive. I don't have to take their pearls to control them." My stomach flopped, thinking back to Theo. "I can make suggestions, twist and pervert their thoughts. My Malice can make them do things. She can worm her way into their souls and make promises she won't keep, for that soul to do horrible things that I want."

"Finally, you've answered the question I've always wondered. Why would Zephyr spend so much time keeping you and me apart? Why does he track your and my every movement? And up until the day you selected me to help you, he forbade me from being the only other person in the room with you."

"Aeden had mentioned Zephyr had kept us apart but never told me the reasons," I replied.

"Once I answer your first question, you'll understand the rest. How much worse it can get with my power. Like you, I don't have to get my hands dirty. One suggestion and they will turn on each other, hordes of them. Your Malice may suggest to one at a time, but my power will force communities to burn each other alive. Together, we're a ticking bomb, where no one lives through our destruction. Together, we would gain the attention of our Gods. Together, we are the worst power in all Elphame. All will notice, not just the Gods. Power attracts the more powerful, and we do not want to stand face to face with those more powerful than us, Perdi."

"The more powerful can get in line. I'm already serving two Crow sentences. There's got to be a rule about a third," I replied and brushed it off to deal with when we weren't being held captive by lunatics. "Your power must come in handy on the battlefield."

He shook his head. "I don't risk opening that particular door. Eventually, I'll never be able to close it, and I'll need to be hunted…and rightfully so. To use the darkest parts of magick is similar to when you witches sell your souls for dark spells. Sooner or later, you've sold too much, and your soul is gone, leaving you nothing more than dark power. We're sitting here because of dark magick. I don't ever want to be the one who does this to others. Most Aos Si do not use their magick to its fullest extent because of what we could do if we had no souls to stop us. It's awful enough to take a life. Why make it that much worse? To unleash all I am, I'd be punished for it. I don't want to win bad enough to suffer for it later."

"Have you ever used your power on me?" I asked.

"No. Once, in my cave, you felt it roll by, and just the slightest of touches was enough for you to feel uncomfortable. But you've never been the target of my power. You'd know if you were. You'd remember the terror."

"I wasn't scared of you when we first met. But I was pretty scared when you first found me here. Does that have something to do with your magick?"

"No, it's not magick. Your Malice would have sensed danger whether I used my magick or not. She's that little voice in the back of your head that tells you to step back, to run. When we first met, there was no reason for you to fear me, so you didn't. When I came into the cave, I didn't get a sense that you were scared of me specifically, just scared in general, scared of your memories. But since I'm not part of those twisted dreams and thoughts, your fear is not directed at me. It's not really focused on any one person."

"How do you know?" I asked.

He tapped his nose. "I can smell your fear, but it doesn't grow or diminish with my presence. Thus, I'm not the cause of it."

"I suppose I wasn't really scared of you, merely the entire species of our people, because that's not going to be difficult at all to overcome later." My sarcasm was thick. "Finn, how does it feel after you use your magick on someone? I always feel awful after I eat a soul. It doesn't seem to matter the why behind it. It hurts, no matter what."

"The same as you. Most of us, who still care about where our souls go when we die, don't use the sharp end of our abilities unless we have no other choice. Could you imagine Zephyr eating everyone he didn't like? Or Solas allowing himself the satisfaction of terrifying someone to death just because they pissed him off?"

"Faolan would have died long ago." I smiled.

"And Zephyr would have eaten me the first year of training. I'll be surprised if he doesn't break my legs after this," he added.

"Why would he break your legs?" I asked. "For getting caught?"

"No, Perdi. I have the smell of your flesh on mine. I touched your unclothed body. Last night, I had to lay on top of you to keep you from running away. I had to cover your mouth, whisper sweet nothings in your ear and hold you down with force. No matter the reason,

Zephyr won't like that I touched you or saw you naked."

"Solas would understand," I answered. "He's much more sensible about my survival."

"And as I pointed out, it would be Zephyr that would do the dirty work. In Zephyr's eyes, you are his sister, his blood. To him, it would be like him catching me kissing his mother. Solas, on the other hand, will try to understand, even if he wants to rip off the parts of me that touched you. His heart knows he doesn't own you, but his soul will want for my life. That is just the reality behind getting between oathed mates. But Zephyr won't give a shit," he replied. "I don't think you fully understand how deeply protective he is of you. It overpowers his rational mind. He won't give me a head start like Solas will."

I laughed. "Yeah, Zephyr is not going to like this."

"I don't blame him. You're all he has that is truly his. For the first time in his life, he has a real family, and that, little Crow, is worth killing for. Even though it'll be my ass on the chopping block, I understand. I'd do the same if I smelled one of the other trainees on your skin. You are my friend, my family. I'd kill another if they dishonored you."

"The offer still stands. You can hide behind me when Solas and Zephyr come calling."

"Eat, drink, rest and collect what bits of Elphame you can. Tomorrow, there will be war." He nudged at my food. "Then, once we're home, you can protect me from Solas and Zephyr."

I ate what he had brought and didn't complain that it tasted like eating a branch. But the water was crisp and cooled the rawness in my throat. Sleep came and went, but each noise woke me before I could sleep deeper. This was too close to my memories of being on the run in Elphame for me to relax. Finn settled in behind me and pulled me into his body. The shadows blanketed us both. If anything came for us, the shadows would alert us and do their best to hold them off for us to run.

"Zephyr will break both of our legs for this," I whispered as I tucked deeper into his arms. I was safe there, in a land I very much did not. Sometimes the illusion was enough.

"At least you have a chance against him. He won't hurt you."

I laughed. "Do you know how many times he's knocked me out?"

"Lucky you, you'll be unconscious for it," Finn teased back.

"Thank you for coming after me," I finally said.

"I want hazard pay for guarding you." He laughed and tucked his face into the back of my head. "You're welcome, little Crow."

"Stop calling me that," I replied.

"Would you rather me go back to calling you a little queen?" he asked.

"No," I answered and left it at that.

"Would you rather fight Faolan or Oisin?" Finn asked and changed the subject.

I laughed. "Oisin."

"Really? I think I'd pick Faolan."

"Not me. You see how calm Faolan is? Imagine when that calm exterior comes crashing down," I answered. "Don't you remember him in the dungeons with Theo? If Oisin wouldn't even stay in the room, I don't think I would want to see who Faolan could become."

"Exactly. I was there. I had a front-row seat. It's not worth winning unless you have to work for it. Everything else is just beating someone up."

"Would you rather fight Zephyr or me?" I asked.

"Zephyr. At least it's only one beating. If I pick you, I have to fight Zephyr, Solas, Nix, Orrian and the entire Aos Si after," he replied. "Worst of all, I'd have to deal with your little Sluagh and all his people. There are thousands of the bloody things."

"Milo." I laughed. "He is the one I leashed, and his mother tried to eat me."

"You named it?"

"Yes, and before you tell me they can't be pets, he's mine," I answered. "Finn, thank you for this…for being here. Not just the failed rescue, but not leaving me here, even after I told you to."

"Failed rescue? I think I'm doing an okay job. I could have let go of your hand and saved myself a witch threatening to cut off my delicate bits. Carver was not the first to notice my birthmark." He laughed at my jab. "You're welcome. It costs a lot to leave your old life behind, only to be dragged back to it. No one should have to pay that cost alone."

"I didn't willingly decide to leave my old life behind."

"Not many of us do, little Crow. Everyone you know didn't make that choice willingly. It was thrust upon us," he answered. "It's how we understand the agony of it all. You never forget what could have been and never stop wondering where you'd be in life if only you were given a choice."

"If you could pick anything else to be, what would you choose?" I asked.

"I don't think I'd want to be anything else, not anymore. Once, I thought to become Aos Si was a death sentence. And even though I fought to join and remain, it was hard as hell, and I thought about quitting more times than not. But it isn't that way anymore. I can still have the life I want."

"Will you ever leave Aos Si?"

"Perhaps, one day, when I wish to have a family of my own. Until then, I'm with the family I want. How about you?"

I smiled. "I once wanted to be a Guardian of the Gate but ended up as a Crow. Weird how things change."

"They didn't really change. You just took a more painful route, but you still protected your people in the only available ways you had. In essence, you're very much a Guardian of the Gate and have done a hell of a lot more than anyone else has to protect mortals."

"They don't appear very grateful." I laughed.

"They never are. You can save hundreds, and one of them always comes back to tell you how you could have done it better." His sigh ended in a yawn. "Get some rest, Perdi, because this won't be any easier tomorrow."

I didn't sleep any deeper with Finn tucked behind me, with his back toward any coming threats, but I did feel safer, which was a commodity in our current situation. I knew, from how relaxed his body was, he felt the same way. He knew I'd help him as quickly as he would, me.

I hadn't slept for long before the shadows stirred over us. "Shadows are coming back. They have Carver with them."

"What do you mean, they're back?" I asked.

At the mouth of our den, we watched the shadows, who had left earlier, return in a swirl of darkness. They joined with those who had remained, dropping Craver at Finn's side. The fairy looked as tired as I felt.

"We can't get out of Whitwick. Whatever force they have in front of the Gate, we are not strong enough to pass," the shadows explained. "It doesn't feel like a Gate, but it is a wall without any cracks for us to worm through."

"None of us can get through," Carver said.

"How far are we from Whitwick?" I asked.

"A day, maybe two, walking," he answered.

All my hope began to leak from me. I leaned forward and breathed deeply, waiting for the initial shock of it all to pass. My mind swirled with dark and defeating thoughts. A wave of nausea gripped my stomach, and I swallowed my need to be sick. If we couldn't get out, there would be no one coming in. I told myself to calm down, to think it through, that I had faced horror before and had come out on top. But I'd had the use of Magick and had the power of the Dark Court armies at my back. Now, I was a broken and beaten Crow, without magick or Malice.

"What the hell do we do?" I whispered, more for myself. I stood and closed my eyes. "All right, this is okay. We'll be okay. We've all faced worse and been hunted by better."

"We have many ideas, but none you will appreciate," the shadows answered.

"Death, war, killing?" I asked.

"Yes," they answered. "None of us are walking out of here without killing for it."

"So be it," I replied, resolved to do what it took to get home. "If burning Whitwick to the ground is the only way we go home, let's light some fires."

Finn stood at the mouth of the cave and grinned. "To war, we go. But if we plan to win a war against an entire population of witches and mortals, we'll need a few things. We need supplies, food, shelter and energy. We cannot plan without gathering what we will need first."

The shadows twisted in front of us. "We will go for supplies. We can move through Whitwick easily, undetected. You all will be caught and will end up back in the warded space. We have our doubts about a second escape from that prison."

"We must keep moving, rather than stay put and be found. Keep them chasing us. They'll tire long before we will," Finn said. "I'd rather not be tucked back here with little maneuverability. We'll have better luck out there."

"I agree," I replied and motioned to the shadows. "Can you find the others who were with us, and tell them to stay put. Once we have a plan, we'll meet at the ridge outside Whitwick, and we'll all go together."

"Go east. Stay close to the water. You can feel Elphame a little stronger at the water," the shadows replied. "We'll find you there."

"If you can feel Elphame there, can we use the river to get home?" I asked.

"No, it doesn't go into Elphame. But the witches cannot ward the magick the water soaks up near the Gate," they replied, and I nodded. Hope was a difficult emotion to quash. "Warding water is impossible. It doesn't stand still long enough to place a spell upon it. It won't be a path home, but it will help us create our own way."

With Finn in the lead, we headed out after the shadows, them going one way, us going a different one. I had slept through the night in sporadic bursts, which left me feeling like I hadn't had a wink of sleep. I moved through the trees as quietly as I could, but my legs were tired, and each step ripped a healing scab from my skin. My nervousness kept me on high alert and made me jumpy. Being without my abilities made my stomach twist in uncertainty. My heart pounded in my chest, and I could hear the beat thump in my ears. If we were in Elphame, I'd have been terrified my pulse would give away our location or the smell of fear that I knew clung to my skin. But in the mortal realm, we were no louder than the wind and couldn't be tracked as easily by humans...witches or not.

Chapter Nine

Being cut off from magick didn't hinder Finn in the least. He marched as though he was a force on his own and wasn't dragging a tired and broken Crow behind him. He had to stop a couple of times while I tried to catch my breath. Although I slowed us down, he never mentioned it or rushed me along. He waited, checked my arms for infection and made me take water and food breaks. When I apologized, he acted like he needed the rest as well. He didn't. And I appreciated him all the more for being kind about it. Had he been alone, I imagine he'd already be in Whitwick, eating the villagers.

"Close," Finn whispered and motioned ahead. He had changed our course a few times, leading us to the water by sound alone. "I can hear the water."

"I bet hide-and-seek was a blast with you as a child," I teased.

"What is hide-and-seek?" he asked.

I smiled. "I guess it was just a human game. It's where one player, called the seeker, closes their eyes and counts, while the other players hide. Once the seeker is done counting, they have to find the hiders. The first person to be found is then the seeker, and the last to be found is the winner."

"I can hear your heart beating, Perdi. If I pay close enough attention, I can hear the blood pumping in your veins and your stomach growling. It would be a short game among Fae."

"That's what I meant by my comment... Never mind, Finn." I laughed. "I just meant that your hearing and sense of smell are impeccable."

"Speaking of, maybe you should use some of that water to clean your feet?" he teased.

"You don't exactly smell like roses, Finn," I replied and shoved him forward.

I could smell the water before I could see or hear it. Finn crept ahead first and scouted for any stray mortals who could be hunting. He motioned with his head. The coast was clear. I stepped through the brush to see the calm water twisting through the green land. The top of the water was glassy and sparkled in the sunlight. The shadows were right. I could feel more of Elphame along the banks. I breathed in deeply and my muscles relaxed. A small groan escaped as I drank down the energy in the air. It had been my first clean breath of air since coming to Whitwick. The cuts and scratches on my arms began to mend on their own, with the little bits of magick refilling my soul. Larger wounds would need to wait for me to return to Elphame, and there were many to heal when I got home.

I took the cap off my canteen and used the lid for Carver to drink from. I dipped my bottle into the river and drank two full jugs before I got back to my feet. Carver stood along the riverbank with his arms wide open. I watched the remaining parts of his wings grow back, little by little, as his little body filled up with magick. At first, his expression was pained as he healed the trauma of the witches. Slowly, the pain ended, and he smiled from ear to ear. Although his people were utterly terrifying when they smiled, with too many pointed teeth and wide mouths, it was beautiful to see today.

"Oh, yeah! Look at these suckers!" Carver lifted off the ground and flicked his wings. He twirled in the air and snapped his wings like fingers.

"They look mighty fine, Carver," I replied.

His laughter made me grin as wide as possible. I knelt beside him and pulled the lingering Elphame energy from the air, but I couldn't fill myself up like I would have if we were in Elphame. Carver needed only a drop of what I would need. I flattened myself on the ground and dipped my arms into the crisp water. It wasn't cold, but it certainly wasn't bath water. I washed the old blood from my hands and arms and, finally, from my face. It wasn't perfect, but it felt pretty damn close to it. Finn sat a few feet away and did the same thing, washing off the remains of torture and those who would have come looking for us.

"At least the water here doesn't scare me," I joked, then motioned downriver to the coming shadows. "That was fast. They're back."

The shadows curled over the water like horses in a full gallop and crawled up the bank. They spat a bag at my side. I dried my hands on my dirty pants, scowling at the filth my hands came away with. I opened the bag and dug through the contents—weapons, knives, a small book, food, bandages and a glass jar.

"Did you find the others?" I asked.

"Yes. They've found a few stray Fae who have been hiding out. They're all waiting on your signal for invasion," the shadows replied. "In Whitwick, there are three powerful witches—sisters who are descendants, they claim, of the Darkmore line. They are who the others are following, other witches. But the other witches feel empty. They can say the words, but there is no power within them. They were the ones who brought the Mages with them, most of whom were killed in Elphame. But together, they're casting spells to keep Elphame at bay, cursing a wall rather than creating a Gate."

I shook my head. "I'm the last Darkmore. There are no lines of sisters. We are all only children since the Gate was created. No Darkmore has ever risked having more than one child, or they'd be used by the Fae or hunted by mortals."

"We know this, but no one else seems to remember your history. I think the town's people are desperate enough to believe anything that gives them a morsel of hope. The witches are powerful, though. Together, they are almost as powerful as you were the day you came to Elphame—but not as powerful as you've become. We guess that is how they are blocking Elphame."

I picked up an empty glass jar and inspected it. "What is this?"

"We took it from the witch's cabin, where they were keeping you. It feels of Elphame, so we took it," they answered. "We thought you'd want it. It's the only unopened jar."

Finn smelled the jar and pulled back. "It is spooled magick. It's yours, Perdi. It smells of you, but it also smells of something more—something I don't think you should open since no one else was brave enough to."

"What do you think would happen if I did?" I asked as I was opening it. I peered into the empty jar, looking for monsters. "Nothing, apparently."

My first deep breath left, as I had held it in wait for horrible things to sprout from the jar. My second one shuddered from my lungs, and I dropped the jar, shattering it on the rocks. I fell to my knees, my chest void of air as I was slapped with the full force of raw power, like standing in a rainstorm and being struck by lightning. Power pushed down my throat and rolled from my head to my toes, burning with each inch it gained. Once the pain peaked, I finally felt my Malice stir in my stomach. They had bottled the one part of me they couldn't use for the Gate. She answered only to me, and even that was a pretty big stretch. She, like me, couldn't be tortured into doing something she didn't want to do.

"Oh, crap," I whispered. "This is going to hurt."

"We wondered where she went," the shadows called out to me as I curled into a ball.

"What the hell is that?" Finn asked.

"It is her Malice," the shadows answered. "Perdi was born a Darkmore Witch. But with her Fae blood and her Malice, she is a Soul-Eater."

"It feels like…" Finn whispered.

"Zeph," I answered.

"Pure rage." Finn finished his sentence. "Jesus, she feels worse than Zephyr on a bad day."

I closed my eyes and let my Malice drag me into that pool of warm rage. The deeper I went, the more tired I became, and I welcomed the respite from the world. My Malice held me down as she got reacquainted. There was nothing gentle about her touch—not today, not ever. At first, it felt like she was holding my head underwater. And like drowning, once I stopped struggling, it was peaceful. She lulled me into the darkness of my soul. And I slept in the slumber of my most familiar emotion...rage. For the first time since being Taken again, I wasn't homesick.

"Perdi?" Solas looked up. He stood in a field in front of the Gate. He was dreaming. I could feel him tossing and turning in bed. *Wisps of darkness slipped from his fingertips, searching for me.* I could feel his desperation as clearly as the pillows under his head. "Perdi!"

I tried to step farther into his dream but was tethered to the mortal realm. It felt like the magick of the Gate blocked everything, including our dream state. Nothing I screamed made it through to him. It echoed around me as if it were bouncing around in a glass box. *Solas yelled my name repeatedly, but all I could do was watch him twist in circles, looking for me. In his dream, he stood alone in the field of the courtless lands, screaming out to me. I watched as the edges of the dream darkened and faded just enough for me to panic. I clawed to hold on.*

"Hold on, Perdi!" Solas could feel my nails gouge at his soul, but he never pulled away, even though it would have hurt something fierce. Instead, he begged me to stay.

Zephyr stepped through and touched Solas' shoulder. "You're dreaming, Solas."

"She's here. I can feel her." Solas spun and grabbed onto Zephyr's collar and shook him violently. Spittle flung from his lips. "Don't you fucking dare take me from my dream, Zephyr. She's here, damn it! I can smell her. I can feel her

touch. I feel her trying to hold on to my dream. I know every feather on her wings and feel each of them against my soul."

Zephyr pulled Solas' hands from his throat and backed away, his face pained. "She's not here, Solas. I don't know where she is, but we'll find a way, I swear to you..." Zephyr tilted his head and breathed in my scent. "Little Crow?"

I couldn't answer. I tried to call out to them, but they heard not a word. I felt a twinge inside my stomach, his pearl. My Malice had hogged all my pearls inside her, guarding them, protecting them. I could feel Zephyr on the other end of his pearl, realizing that my pearl, inside him, was alive and well. He gripped his stomach and smiled.

"Perdi, where are you?" Solas asked, spinning in circles to find me. "Tell me where you are!"

Zephyr opened his eyes and breathed calmly. "I feel you fading, little Crow. Do not waste your energy on this dream."

"No!" Solas screamed. "Don't send her away. She's all by herself. Zephyr, please, don't let her go."

"It's okay, Solas. I can feel Finn beside her, as well as one of Orrian's best, Carver, and some of the shadows. She's not alone out there. I promise you. Do not ask her to waste the energy she has to stay here. She has so very little of it, and she'll need it to get home." Zephyr touched Solas' arm again, and Solas quieted. "Perdi, get to the Gate. We can't pass through the magick. Not even the Sluagh can get through. You must break the spells on the Gate. It is time, little Crow, to become all you are, all you're hiding, to get home. We will come. On this, I swear to you. We will eat that fucking Gate to get to you. Tell Finn it is time to take off his mask. I will need the Finn of old. Together, you will show the world why the Gods made the mistake of birthing you both in the same lifetime."

"I will come, Perdi. I swear on my life I will find you. Just hold on a little longer. Please, hold on," Solas cried, and although I couldn't reach him, I felt his pain pluck against my ribs as his pearl cried with him. I knew exactly what he was feeling, fear and guilt. How everything else didn't matter. I had thought the same things when they were taken from me, and I had to wage war to get them back from my enemies.

I sat straight up from a dead sleep and almost brained myself on Finn's forehead. He jerked back, his hands dropped from my shoulders as though he had been trying to wake me, and I hadn't moved until now. The look of worry on his face was endearing. Finn may have been many horrible things to others, but not everyone got to see the Finn I saw.

"We have to get to the Gate," I blurted out in a rush of hot wind. I wiped the tears from my eyes, my heart still raw from what I felt within Solas' dream.

"How? Then what?" the shadows asked.

"We do our absolute worst," I answered. "Leave no one alive."

Finn smelled the air. "You saw Solas or Zephyr?"

"I could see them both in Solas' dream. They couldn't see or hear me, but they could feel me. Zephyr could finally feel my pearl. He told me to get to the Gate and break the spell holding Elphame back. He said it was time for me to become all I am."

Finn smiled. "Well, won't this be fun? Me, a Crow and a bunch of wee folk, waging war on the mortal world. I can't see how this isn't going to hurt like a bitch."

I grabbed onto his hand. "Do your worst, Finn. Zeph told me to tell you that it's time to take off your mask. He said he needs the Finn of old."

"Fuck." He released a shuddered breath. "This is going to hurt so bad, little Crow."

"I know."

"No, I don't think you do." He crouched down, meeting my eyes. Behind his usual excitement for war, I could see fear. "To hear of my power is much different than seeing what it does with your own eyes. I am so much worse than you think I am. What I can do is awful, Perdi. It won't be us fighting an entire realm. It will just be death. When I step foot into Whitwick and my power rolls over their homes…they will kill each other for me. I won't bloody my hands here — mortals will do it for me — but my soul will bleed for what I'm about to do. You wondered if someone was a bigger monster than you were. *I* am the creature that hunts monsters bigger than you. I am what the Gods release for war. And together, we will have to answer for what we do. Are you ready for that?"

"No," I replied.

"Neither am I. But I want you to know the cost. If we do this, not only will we face judgment for it, but you'll be showing both realms that there are two of you…two Soul-Eaters. As for me, I've never unleashed all I am like this. I've never had free rein to do my worst. I don't know what will happen, and together, we'll suffer for it."

"We will kill pieces of ourselves today so that we all will have a tomorrow, because that is the cost of survival when you can eat the world," I answered. "We'll worry about tomorrow, tomorrow. Just know, Finn, I won't leave your side tomorrow because of what I will see today. I will still love you tomorrow. I hope you can say the same about me."

"Thank you. It wouldn't be worth it if I burned away everything good in my life just to have one more day alone." He held out his hand and pulled me to my feet. "There is nothing you can show me I haven't already seen or wouldn't do myself."

I looked out of the hills and felt a resolve settle in my bones. I didn't want to do what I knew we'd do, but too many of our people were counting on Finn and me to get them home. They had come into a foreign land for me, not knowing if they'd live or die, and suffered insurmountable pain in my name. They'd left the protection of Elphame to find me. And even with the freedom they now had, they still waited for me rather than seeking out their own safety. In their broken and bloodied state, they were willing to fight to the end beside me. It would be a cold day in hell that I'd leave them to suffer another day in this realm. We were going home — or we would die trying.

"To get our people home, to carry the wounded back into Elphame, to honor those who came for me and died, I'll split myself wide open. Will you?"

"I'll do so much worse, Perdi, for our people," he replied. "To war, we go, little Crow."

"Stop calling me that."

"As you wish, little Crow."

Chapter Ten

We moved with ease, from location to location, throughout the rest of the fading day. Elphame energy returned back to our bodies as we inched our way closer to Whitwick. My Malice ate up every kernel of power and saved it for what was coming. She was starved of energy, hungry for retribution and itched to be let loose on those who had harmed us. Through her, the memories of what had happened to me while I slept hit home and burned like an inferno in my stomach. I remembered every detail with perfect clarity. Every laugh and insult, the sounds of my people screaming out in pain, drove me forward with purpose.

One final move left to make gave us focus and willed us to become the monsters we tried so hard not to be. With Finn at my side, it reminded me of when we had been together on Satyr Island. And like last time, we were hunting an entire population of people, and for the same reasons, to save those we loved. As we walked, Finn whispered to himself, trying to convince his soul that he would be okay. He would still have a family come tomorrow. I gripped his hand and told myself the same thing.

We collected the remaining Fae, those who had come to find me and those who hadn't made it back before the Gate closed. Over the course of two days, we had six dozen Fae, all ranging in size but none bigger than Nix. After spending a year with the Fae, I knew their size meant nothing. Nix was small but a war machine — and feared by most. His people were known for eating the eyelids off their enemies to terrify those who would think to avenge their deaths. That alone made me shiver at the thought of having six dozen who would do the same.

With my Malice tucked back inside, the shadows rolling across the ground, both eating the wisps of power in the air, we made our way back to Whitwick. The last leg of the journey was met with anxiety, fear and the desire to skip a war and dig our way out. None of us wanted to do what had to be done. Revenge was sweet, but going home without having to kill for it was sweeter. Finn gave each of us directions. We all had a part to play, and Finn would make sure the mortals would feel the sting in every corner of Whitwick. Our army may be small, but it meant nothing — not when it was a Fae army coming.

"This is it," I whispered to them all. We stood in the forest just above where my old home had been. "Children live, their mothers live. Those who run, as long as they are not witches or Mages and have no blood on their hands, may live. Everyone else who waged war on Fae, who tied us down and took our magick and lives dies. Those who stand in our way die. The witches and Mages don't get a free pass for any reason. They are what is holding that Gate closed. Am I clear? When we are finished, they will think twice about knocking on our doors again."

"My lady." A gnome half of Nix's size bowed. "We will see you on the other side of hell."

"Do you all remember what to do and where you go?" I asked and received all nods. "Stay in the shadows. We will use their fear of the fog to our advantage. I'll see you all when the dust settles. All of you come home. When you can no longer fight, or you're too injured, go back to the Gate and wait. Those who need help or are hurt, you will drag them to the Gate and protect them as best you can. Do not risk yourselves any more than you have to. There will be no heroes today…only death. And I don't want to carry your dead bodies home, not after getting this far."

"I will see you on the other side of sacrifice and sin." Finn's voice was a whisper, and he was gone in a breeze that chilled my soul.

"Find my father," I told the shadows, and they blasted from the forest in a fog that twisted my stomach.

I waited for the first and second waves to leave. They'd wage war from within the fog made of shadows. I paced and waited until the bells tolled over Whitwick. When the screaming started, the rest of us ran toward a very likely death. The streets were covered in fog and Fae. It was nothing more than shadows, but memories had a way of terrorizing you, convincing you of other things. The first pang of guilt tried to settle in, that I'd use their fears against them, as Finn had suggested. But the moment I saw the wee folk fighting against those who had tortured them, the guilt was gone as quickly as it had come.

Six dozen wee folk held Whitwick in the grip of horror. And there, I unleashed my Malice and held nothing back. We all moved from house to house. Those who stood against us, who smelled of torture on their flesh, fell as we left. There was no middle ground. They'd discover that they drained our mercy along with our blood and magick. There couldn't be, not for what they had done to us. I ate their souls as I moved on to the next, spooling their energy. If I couldn't take it from Elphame, I'd take it from the people who'd brought us here.

In the middle of the street, the hag from my prison stood with my bloodied father at her feet. I stepped toward her. She pulled a blade from her pocket and motioned down to my father. I knew she'd end his life if I stepped another foot forward. I nodded my head and stood still. She smiled, but it wasn't a friendly smile. I memorized every inch of her face, from her eyes to her lips. Not a single line went unnoticed. If she did get away, I'd never forget her. Her mouth moved, but I heard nothing but the swoosh of my own pulse.

"Perdita." She called my attention back to her. "I expected you days ago."

I breathed in her magick and shook my head, as if disappointed in her stupidity. Her pearl, locked in a rusted cage, was dark as night. Her power was just as black, but it would never best mine on my worst day. She had forgotten that her strength and power over me had come from locking me in a Fae trap. But I was no longer caged. I was no longer her victim to control through pain.

"I would run if I were in your shoes. I would run as fast and as far as I could," I said, my voice void of everything but hate.

"You are not in my shoes. So, what does it matter?" she asked. She leaned forward and grabbed my father by his hair, jerking his face to hers. "I will leave unharmed or your father will die."

"I wouldn't do that if I were you," I spoke calmly, even though my rage seethed inside like a beast out of breath. "It will be the last thing you ever do. Do you understand me?"

She pressed the knife against my father's neck. "You are in no place to make threats, Crow. Stop this, or I will take his life. Do *not* force my hand."

"We didn't start this, you did, when you took from Elphame. Nothing is free, witch. You took us, and now you pay the price for taking that which is not yours to have," I replied. "I warned you this would happen. I told you on that first day we spoke, you would fail and die for it. I gave you the chance to survive. I gave this entire goddamn realm the chance to live. But you chose this ending. I didn't. And now you've sentenced yourself, your sisters and all of Whitwick to an ending worse than any Taking."

If we stopped, this would only continue. We would keep dying at each other's hands until there was no one left to care. But if I didn't, my father would die. With my father at her feet, I knew what was going to happen. He glanced at me once and nodded. He knew his life was over the moment he stepped through the Gate. I could feel his pearl from feet away, and he was saying goodbye.

"I love you," he whispered. "Kill them, or they'll never stop coming for you."

The witch smiled. She knew her fate was sealed, just as my father's was. She just hadn't crawled into her grave yet. She would die regardless of my decision, so she made it for me. She pushed the knife into my father's chest, and I blew open with rage as I watched him hit the ground and blood pool on the dirt. The fog that rolled around her feet crawled up her legs, slicing her flesh as they moved. The first hint of her scream was eaten as the shadows forced their way down her throat. When the witch landed in a heap beside my father. I drew my blade and leaned over her.

"You should have killed me then drained me of my blood, you foolish witch." I pushed the knife into her heart and tore her mind to shreds with my Malice. I greedily pulled her soul from her dying body. "Now you'll live forever in the one land you hated enough to kill for."

The shadows poured out of her chest wound, gaping it into a bloody window. "Your father." The shadows rolled over him.

I dropped the hag in the dirt and fell to my knees. "Dad, wake up." I jerked on his arm. "Please, Dad."

"He is gone, Perdi," they whispered to me. "He was gone before he landed."

"No!" I screamed and felt the earth tremble under my knees. I couldn't contain my pain. It was everywhere, in every breath I took, every push of blood through my veins. I stood, grief dripping from my eyes. My hands shook with the need to strangle the life out of that witch all over again. I regretted putting the knife in her heart for no other reason than not being able to kill her slowly for what she had done. "No one survives this hellhole."

"Where are you going?" the shadows asked.

I breathed in the air and could smell the dark magick. I had one purpose. I closed my eyes and tracked the magick that had locked me in a cage, had killed my people and were of the bloodline of the witch I had just killed. Two witches, sisters, running from the terror they had unleashed on the mortal realm with their evil promises—promises they had made, promises they had broken. I let my Malice free and ran behind the two who thought they'd get away. They may have had a head start, but no mortal could outrun Fae. And I'd never let them go. I'd hunt them until my last days, but I'd get them eventually. My grief would outlive them both and would drive me to find them before they died for some other reason. I'd fight fate tooth and nail to be the one to claim their lives.

To break the spell holding back Elphame, I'd have to kill the last two. But now, I'd do it out of pure spite and hate. It had taken me less time to find them than it had for me to get out of bed most mornings. The hags were old. They were slow. They were cocky. They were sure. They thought I wouldn't come for them. They were dead wrong, just as their sister had been. And now the witches would die for what they had done, for what I knew they'd do if they got away. I could read their pearls like an open book. They'd return and come with supporters, far and wide.

Finn stepped into their paths. "I warned you all, and you didn't listen. Now you'll live forever and ever with the very monsters you tried to kill."

They froze, then smiled as though they weren't facing death in a matter of minutes. Finn held them with nothing more than his magick, promising them freedom and pleasure. His power rolled over my arms as I came to a stop. It was calm and loving, like coming home after a long journey after too many years away. It felt how my return to Whitwick should have been. But these witches would get the same thing I had been given—hate, hell, *pain.*

"No!" I yelled. "They will not enjoy this, Finn. You will not take this from me! They suffer, just like we had to. They do not get to die peacefully. None of our people were offered that mercy, and neither will they."

He glanced over their heads, and after a long moment of weighing if he should let me exact my revenge, he nodded but looked sadder for it. Finn pulled back his power and left me to the screams of the witches. I ate their fear and their souls. I swallowed them down and left their bodies for the birds. I emptied their bags and collected their spell books. I smashed the rest on the rocks. I wouldn't leave the roots of their cause on the ground for others to take up in their absence. Everything they were and had become would die today.

I had the shadows to bring me to the warded world we had been held in. I pressed my bloodied hands into the soil and drained the power from the spell. Those who had made the ward were dead. With only my blood holding it firm, I took my magick back. With a deafening pop, the ward fell like a bucket of water tossed into the air.

"Go see if there are any survivors still in there and bring them back. I don't care how feral they are. No more of our people will die here. They come home." I motioned to our once prison. The shadows burst through the field, blanketing the ground and rolling across it like thunder.

They carried back seven, barely alive, wee folk. Wrapped in my pain and shadows, we landed in the middle of Whitwick amid the terror and screams. We left those we found close to the Gate to draw up any energy that escaped. Little by little, I watched wisps of fog roll from the Gate and fill the streets. It stopped once, touching me, only to pull away from my pain and move along to lend a hand to the horrors. I cringed at first, the memories of what the fog represented turning over in my stomach. Today, however, my recoil was replaced by anger and lust for so much more than the fog would ever do.

"Those who have survived our coming have run." Carver came to my shoulder. "I'm sorry, Perdi. We have wrapped your father to be carried home when we leave."

"Those who have run won't get far," I replied. My heart hammered at the thought of losing my dad. This realm had taken both of my parents, and I hated them all the more for it. "Thank you, Carver, for caring for my father."

"The survivors didn't get beyond the field," Finn called out. I watched him walk down the road to meet me. His eyes held the beginnings of a haunt that would terrorize him later. "There are no survivors left in Whitwick, aside from those who got a free pass from you." Finn cleaned his blade. "I have four who were hiding. They smell of your father's blood."

"Who? Where are they?" I asked.

"I saved their fate for you to decide," Finn replied. "The men responsible for the injuries to your father look familiar, from the last time we were here. One, I believe, is named Peter."

"Lead the way, Finn," I answered. He spun, and I followed behind him. It felt like walking through a battlefield in Elphame, bodies everywhere. Those who fell didn't deserve it as much as I wanted them to, but they were also not innocent. They helped torture Fae, torture me. They chose to either remain silent and did nothing to help us – or agreed to it.

For our survival, we chose our lives over theirs. For now, I could live with it. Later, it would crush me. I had done to mortals what Fae had been doing for generations. I took their lives because I didn't deem them deserving of life, because I was stronger, because I could.

"My lady." Finn stepped to the side and presented four men on their knees. They looked like they had suffered weeks of torture, even though they had only sampled minutes with Finn. I had problems with all four men from the very start, and all four had used my father to get to me.

"How did you take my father?" I asked. No one replied. I pointed at Peter and did everything I could to silence the growl in my throat. I had warned him before that if the Fae came, it would end in their deaths. Instead, they brought their deaths into their lands all on their own. "You can answer my question or die here."

"Fuck…" Peter spat blood from his mouth.

"You," I answered.

"Do you want him to want this or not?" Finn asked.

"Not," I answered. "They are the ones who called Elphame into their lands. Let them feel what nightmares they invited to their front doors."

Finn stood behind him, and I watched as Peter's face shifted from bravery to terror. His eyes widened as his mind reeled from whatever thoughts were forced in from Finn. His scream did nothing to me. I had screamed the same way when they'd sliced my arms open and drained me of my blood. Finn slowly ended Peter's life with a blade, while Peter begged and pleaded that he would help me and tell me the truth. I didn't flinch. I felt nothing for taking his life as I smelled his blood mixed with my father's. It was splattered on his clothes.

I moved to the next man. "How did you take my father? Like the chance I gave Peter, you can answer my questions or die here."

His eyes were just as wide as Peter's had been, from watching his friend die at his side. "The witches, they got word to your father. They told him that we were willing to bargain for a new oath. When he came through the Gate, he was taken. The witches used his blood to cast a spell, to pull you here."

"Did you torture him?" I asked.

"Yes," he replied. "You were our enemy as much as we are yours."

"I have no enemies," I replied and turned my back. "All of my enemies are dead."

I walked away to the sounds of them screaming and felt the first seed of guilt I knew would stay and grow. It was the first of so much more to come. I sat on the sidewalk in front of the Gate and waited for the rest of the spell to finally break its hold on it and free the nightmares I knew would come.

"I would have done the same thing." Finn sat beside me.

I nodded. The numbness was starting to fade, letting in the awful reality of what we had done. "Yet it doesn't feel good."

"No, it doesn't," he replied. "But just because it's hard doesn't mean it shouldn't be done."

"You didn't flinch. Neither of us did," I replied.

"Flinching doesn't say much about how easy it is for a person or not. My hand has never wavered, but my soul has. Sometimes it is easier than other times, depending on the reason for my arrival. But tonight, when I'm alone, when it's dark, I'll feel it all, and it'll fucking hurt. I'll hate myself for it…for all of this. But I wanted to live more. I wanted you to live more. I wanted my people to go home again, to see their families, to heal from what was done to them. And I'd have done worse for that to happen," he answered. "Was it easy for you?"

"In the moment, it was easy. Like you, I would have done worse to win," I answered honestly. "Later, though, it won't be. I don't think I'll ever heal from what we did today."

"I'm sorry, little Crow. I'd have done it all myself if I could have," he answered.

I grabbed onto his hand and tucked myself against him. "I'm sorry, Finny…for the memories you'll have tomorrow."

"Finny?" He laughed, and it sounded odd to hear it, with bodies lying face down in the dirt, up and down the streets of Whitwick.

"If you get to call me nicknames, so do I." I smiled. "Later, find me when it gets too dark for you."

He nodded. "Same, Perdi. This is going to hurt, and you'll need someone who feels it with you. No one can take it away, but finding someone who understands makes the shame of it all a little less."

"We wouldn't be Fae if we didn't pay for it," I answered.

"Ain't that the painful truth." Finn released a long and shuddered breath. He leaned forward, his elbows on his knees, and stared at the Gate, waiting.

"What are you waiting for? The spell will die out now that the three witches are dead." I pointed at the Gate, and the shimmer slowly returned.

He shook his head. "Payment. I'm waiting to pay the cost of what we've done. Nothing is free, not even survival. Eventually, we'll be called on the floor for what we've done here, and I'm not looking forward to it."

I nodded. One way or another, the bill would be due, and we'd suffer all over again. "That Gate will eventually be the death of us all."

"It's the rift, not just the Gate, but the tear between worlds. If you want to stop paying for each day, that's where it'll have to end, because that's where it started. To close that, though, that cost will probably kill us all."

"Of course, it's death. Nothing is ever simple in Elphame," I replied.

"Nothing is ever simple in any realm, little Crow."

All of us, those who were tortured at the hands of Whitwick, those we found and those we saved, sat in a row and waited as the spell slowly died. It started at the edges and finally fell like a curtain. The moment it was down, I could feel hell unleash on the streets of Whitwick. We watched as Elphame puked its horrors onto the empty streets of the mortal world. Milo soared through the air, screaming warnings through the body-littered streets, ready and willing to eat anything that moved. But there was no one left to terrify. The Aos Si were the next through the Gate, poised to strike. Nix scurried through the crowd, jumping shoulder to shoulder to finally land at my side and latch onto my arm. I couldn't understand his words through his sobs, but I understood what he meant.

"I missed you, too," I answered and hugged him. It felt like heaven had handed me a cloud, and it settled my soul to feel his love.

Orrian was next, but she didn't come to me. She grabbed Craver and hugged him. I didn't need to hear what they were saying to feel her utter relief he had lived. After a close inspection, she moved to my front. She patted my hand once and nodded. Her face was stained with tears.

"Perdi, I'll see you on the other side. I'm going home to hug my family." Carver tipped his head and left with Orrian.

"Nix, can you help those who helped me?" I asked.

"By chance, did you see a gnome here?" he asked. "He's about half my size, has longer hair and his skin is a brighter shade of green than mine, like new leaves on a tree."

"Yes, there's a few of them kicking around somewhere. Why?"

"My sister's son… He came through to find you. Those of us who were too big couldn't get through," he replied and called out to the gnome in question. "Rex!"

The gnomes all moved forward. The one I had spoken to before we had waged war limped to Nix and grabbed onto his shoulder. "All four of us made it, Uncle."

"Hells bells, your mother would have torched this place if you didn't come home," Nix replied and pulled Rex into his arms for a hug. "Thank you for coming to find Perdi. You bring honor to your family, to the gnomes. History will remember your name."

Rex grinned, beaming with obvious pride. "Thank you, but I don't want to do this again."

"None of us do," Nix replied.

I fully agreed with him. This had been hell for us all. "Nix, can you get the others home, healed, fed and back to their people? They've been through an awful lot.

Finn and I wouldn't have fared nearly as well without them."

Nix nodded. "I'll see you at home, right? You're coming home, yes? You're coming back?"

I saw his reluctance to leave me and his fear of losing me again. "I'm coming back to Elphame, but I may need to take a few days before I can come home. I'm a little beaten up, inside and out."

"Okay," he replied, taking a few more seconds to make sure before leaving my side.

Nix led the group of Fae who had waged war at my side from the sidewalk. The Aos Si cleared a path for them and took a knee as those who gave their very magick to save me passed. They stayed knelt while the wee folk crossed the Gate.

Zephyr stepped to my front and offered me his hand. "You've been busy, little Crow."

I stood and started to dump tiny pearls into his hands. "Take these. Please, take them for me, Zeph." Souls that twisted in my pockets now rested in Zephyr's hands. "I don't want them. Do something with them."

"I can't take them. They're not mine," Zephyr answered.

"And I don't want them!" I screamed at him. All my anger fell out at once. "Please, just take them. I don't care what you do with them, but I can't keep them. I took them, but...I did it because I hated them. Please, Zeph."

"It's okay, Perdi. It'll be okay." He took the souls and tossed them to the shadows behind him. What they'd do with them, I didn't ask. I didn't care. He pulled me into his arms. "This has felt like the longest month of my life."

"It was only a few days for me, Zeph. The shadows kept me unconscious for most of the time, through the bad parts."

"The memories will come back, Perdi. The bad parts always find their way back home," he replied.

"I know," I answered.

"It's going to hurt, all of this."

"Everything hurts. It doesn't matter where I am," I said.

"Perdi..." Solas' voice made me let go of Zephyr and step back.

My heart slammed into my ribs, pounding suddenly and frantically. In the distance, I could hear the bells toll over the mortal lands. The fog crawled over Whitwick. The streets were filled with Fae. I could see the memory playing out in the back of my mind. My back slammed into Finn, and I pushed until I finally ducked behind him. I couldn't breathe. I closed my eyes and told myself to calm down—but everything around me told me differently. If I calmed down, I'd die. If I didn't hide, they'd Take me, and I'd suffer. I could smell the very day I became a Crow.

"It's not real," I whispered to myself. "I'm okay. It's okay. I'm safe. It's not real. This isn't happening."

"Perdi." Solas' voice called to me again.

"Stop, stop, stop," I whispered and covered my ears. "Please, stop." Solas' voice whispered my name, and I screamed. "Shut the fuck up!"

"Sir." Finn put his body in front of mine and held his arms behind him to pull me into his back completely. I gripped his arms as if the world was tilting, and he was the only thing that kept me from falling off. "I'm sorry. I need to ask you to please back up."

"Get the hell out of his way," Zephyr commanded. "And why do you smell like Perdi?"

"I can't. I'm sorry," Finn answered. "What they did to her here, it was…horrible. They made her remember her Taking. What's happening right now in Whitwick reminds her of when this happened to her on the day she was Taken. Look around. This is what it was like for her when she became a Crow. She's scared. It's all a mess…what she remembers. Some of it isn't real. They showed her parts that weren't, but it still feels like it was. They twisted her memory of you all. She remembers Solas doing horrible things to her and letting others do even worse. She remembers the dead king and Solas allowing him to force Perdi to his room. It's not her fault. The witches did this to her."

"It's okay," Solas answered. "Perdi, it's all right. I'm backing up. I won't touch you. No one will touch you. No one will come near you. Where do you want to go? Finn will take you wherever you want to go. No one will stop you. No one will follow you. You are safe with Finn. He kept you alive, Perdi. He is safe."

"Home. Take me home," I said.

"To the Dark Courts?" Finn asked.

"The island," I answered.

"What island?" Finn asked.

Chapter Eleven

Finn sat with me on the front steps of Zephyr's island home and watched the sun set and stars come out. We didn't say much in the first few hours, but once the scab was pulled off, we shared the worst parts of who we were, the parts we didn't like to say out loud. We talked about being in Whitwick, the horrors of it all and what we each did to make sure we all came home. Finn, like me, could kill without flinching, but our souls suffered afterward every time. He spoke of the Gods and Goddesses noticing what we had done and his fear that they would strike us down. I didn't think they gave a shit about what we did to each other. They never had before, and I doubted very much that they'd care today.

He stayed with me for the first week on the island. Neither of us wanted to face the rest of the world. He helped me recut the wounds on my arms and the symbols on my body to heal with salve and Elphame magick. Of all the things that bothered me, having hideous scars was at the top of my list and the only thing I had the power to control. It hurt, but not nearly as much as everything else weighing on my soul. In turn, I did the same for the mutilations he had suffered at the hands of the witches. Some would scar and some would fade. The same could be said of the memories we'd carry of our time in Whitwick.

Side by side, we comforted each other until the numbness went away, leaving behind raw and tattered souls. For that healing to come, I needed space. I needed to rebuild myself and also needed to be alone to do so. I couldn't be put back together by others this time. I also couldn't face the world yet, but I could start little by little. It wouldn't be what the others wanted, the journey I'd have to take to find myself again, but like the Gods, I didn't care about what others needed or wanted. Healing was something I'd do for myself, and damn everyone else if they didn't understand. I had done enough for everybody else. Now it was time to do what I needed for myself.

I had Finn take me from the island to my father's house. There, Milo helped me dig a grave for my father. I didn't hold a service. I said my piece and placed him in the earth with an apple tree over him. Milo stayed, patrolled the yard and slept on the front porch. During the day, I cleaned the house and packed away my father's belongings. At night, when the pain was more than I could stand, my childhood bedroom filled with darkness and shadows. Tucked inside was the only way my heart would stop hammering. I knew Solas and Zephyr had come, and even as I battled against memories that I knew weren't real, they still took turns watching over me from a distance. Inch by inch, they stepped closer each day, but never enough for me to fear them. They didn't pester, and they didn't rush me. They simply loved me in ways I could handle.

The wounds of my Taking as a Crow were as fresh as they had been the day it had happened, and it felt like I was bleeding all over the place. I felt out of place again. I wasn't mortal enough to live in a world that hunted who I had become, but I was still too human to survive what Elphame brought my way. I was caught between two worlds, and those worlds kept colliding, with me in the middle being torn up. I wanted to be stronger, to be like Solas or Zephyr, but I also hated the idea of being so used to digging graves that my muscles no longer tired.

The night my mind finally broke, I ran. I ran as hard and fast as I could. I stood in the middle of the forest and screamed into the night. The fire in my stomach poured into the earth and burned a patch of land around me. Milo paced, blanketing the fire under his feet with his energy before I torched the entire forest. He stood guard when Faolan came to see why I was in his land, screaming loud enough for everyone in his territory to wake, afraid. When Solas stepped out of the shadows, Faolan stepped away. They exchanged glances but didn't speak to each other. Faolan nodded and left Solas alone with me. Milo stepped to the side and let Solas pick me off the ground. He carried me back to my father's house, and that was the last time I ran. There was nothing I could run from and nowhere I could run to that would take away my pain. I couldn't escape who I had become, and truthfully, I didn't want to be anyone else. I just wanted to stop being punished for being who I was.

A month passed without me being bothered by a single care. The world could burn around me, but I knew no one would let the flames touch me. This house was my in-between, and I craved the calmness of my childhood home. My father was gone from the world, and that hurt would never fully leave. But everywhere I looked, I could see him and hear his gentle voice. Here, within the fondest memories of my life, I could let myself heal from the wounds that had ripped me away from those moments I loved. The memories that ate at me every night didn't sink their teeth nearly as deep inside my in-between. It wasn't perfect, but it helped. And those who loved me understood.

Reading on the deck, Finn came with another load of food. Milo came around from the back of the house with a warning growl. From the bushes, a dozen little dragons came out of hiding, smoke billowing from their mouths. They, like Milo, protected the yard and me.

I glanced up once. "Hello, Finny."

"Stop calling me that." Finn set the crate of food down and didn't approach. "They're meeting at Blood and Bones tomorrow to discuss the fate of the Gate."

I shrugged. "And? Is there a point in telling me?"

"And I thought you'd want to be there. They will be debating the fate of your people."

I shook my head and huffed a small laugh. "They're not my people. And no, I don't want to be there. I don't care what they're discussing. It has nothing to do with me anymore."

"How long do you plan to hide here?" he asked.

"Until I die?" I looked over my book. "How long do you plan on coming here?"

"Until you die, I suppose," he answered. "Although Soul-Eaters live three times longer than most other Fae do."

"Maybe you'll luck out, and I'll die sooner. I'm pretty confident you'll outlive me."

"I doubt Zephyr would allow that," he answered.

"Zephyr commands *you*. He doesn't command *me*," I countered. "Run along, Finny. And tell your commander to stop sending me fucking potatoes. I don't like them."

"I think I'll have my lunch first," Finn replied. Milo growled again, but Finn sat on the ground with his white lunch bag. "Do you want my apple?"

"No. I have my own. There's an apple tree planted over my dead father." I stood and left him outside. Through the front window, I watched him coax Milo to his side with promises of food. Finn and Milo finally sat ten feet apart, with Finn tossing Milo hunks of meat. He always found a way to get the beast to calm down enough to sit beside him. Milo, it appeared, could be bought with a roast sandwich. From his bag, Finn pulled out a bunch of grapes and tossed them to the dragons, who took them and returned to their bush. *Traitors, the lot of them.*

"What are you doing?" I finally came back out.

"You know that Sluagh eat meat, right? He can't live off fruit and vegetables like the dragons can," Finn answered. "If you're going to keep him with you, you need to take care of him. You may be fine with rotting away here, but he doesn't deserve to rot with you."

"I'm not keeping him here," I replied. "He won't leave. I tried to tell him and his dragons to go home. They flew to the caves and came right back with more dragons."

Finn stood. "Milo and his thunder are here for the same reason I come."

"Which is?"

"To keep you alive. They sense your pain and won't leave you alone in it," Finn replied. "Each time I come, I'm scared I will find you hanging from a rope or drowned in your tub."

I rolled my eyes. "I don't plan on killing myself."

"You don't plan on living, either," he replied. "It hurts, but the hurt doesn't stop because you will it away. Nothing in life is that easy."

"You sound like Zephyr." I crossed my arms.

"*Zeph*...you always call him Zeph," Finn replied and stood to face me. "Now, he is *my* commander. And Solas, he's *my* king and not yours. What am *I* to you now? Am I still your friend? Or did I leave half my soul behind in that goddamn place for a stranger?"

"Yes, you're my friend." I sat on the steps and stared beyond him to the forest. "Once, I thought of explaining this to you, that I owed you some sort of reason for why I've shut out the world. But I don't owe you my truths. I don't owe you anything."

"Respectfully, like hell you fucking don't," he answered. "I risked the punishment of the Gods and Goddesses to help you."

I smiled and chuckled. "Look around, Finny. Your Gods don't give a shit about us. If they had, neither me nor you would be standing here today, bruised and scarred from too many years of this hell."

"But I care. I burned off my soul for you. It's taken weeks for my nightmares to stop. I did that for you, to get you home. I became the very thing I promised myself I'd never become, and I did that for you because I love you, and you said you love me. You promised me that you'd still love me the next day. You said I was your family." His voice hitched in his throat. He teetered between anger and pain. "You pretend like you're the only one who suffered. We all did. We all were tortured. And we all lost those we love, our people, to that place. Don't tell me you owe me nothing. You owe me your willingness to live, because that life is what I gave my soul to save."

"I do love you deeply. And I'm so utterly thankful for what you did to help bring our people and me home. But I'm not built like you. I can't just muster anymore. I know you don't understand, and I'm sorry for that."

"Then muster for Carver, who let them cut off his goddamn wings for you. Muster for the pixies who were branded for you. They're walking around with those fucking symbols burned into their bodies. The wee folk were tortured for you. Elphame sent their best, knowingly, to their deaths to find you. I've yet to see you thank their people for their sacrifice. They died to bring you home, and you've yet to even see where they came from and who they left behind. That is not the Perdi I followed into hell. That is not the Crow others gave their lives for."

His words hurt more because there wasn't a lie to be found among them. But that was often the case with truth. It always hurt the most. "I know. I didn't say the road that I'm walking isn't selfish. I know others gave their lives in the most horrific of ways. I haven't forgotten about them. I couldn't, even if I wanted to. I hear them screaming and begging for death every time I go to sleep at night. I remember them all, even though I wish I didn't." I tried to find words to make him understand, but each time I tried, I was empty of reasons. "This isn't about you all. It's about me. I can't worry about everyone else because I'm worrying about myself. And for now, that's all I can muster. It doesn't have to be a good reason for anyone but myself. I want it to be. I wish I had this noble cause behind what I'm doing, but I don't. I'm truly empty of care for anyone other than myself. I'm sorry it hurts. I'm sorry you don't feel my love. I'm sorry that it's selfish, but I can't fix myself while I'm helping everyone else. I can't break myself in two like that…not anymore."

"I've tried to be understanding. I've tried to be your friend when I thought you needed one. Tell me what you need, and I'll do it."

"Perhaps, Finn, that is not what I need right now," I answered. "This isn't about what you can do for me. It's about me and what I can do for myself."

"I don't think you know what you need," he replied. "I think you're sitting here trying to find the reasons for what happened. There aren't any reasons good enough. Bad shit happens to good people all the time. That is the way of the world."

"My peace is more important to me than driving myself to understand why it happened the way it did, why it happened to begin with and why it happened to me. And explaining it to you isn't on my list of things to do. For now, I'm content with sitting here on this doorstep, reading a book I read as a child, in a world that took that childhood away."

"You are caught between those two worlds and want to fit into one of them. You won't. You never will, and it's time to let go of that. You are too much of one for the other, and you are more and less at once. You were never fully mortal or fully Fae, and you straddled both worlds and were punished for it. You are a Soul-Eater who can't manage to keep her own soul in one piece."

"I'm so glad you've come for a pep talk. Tell Zephyr I don't need it." I shook my head. "I don't need his bloody chats or soothing soul talk. And I especially don't need his messages delivered through you."

Finn barked a laugh. "He's told me to leave you alone, lest I wish to be down a soul."

"Maybe you should listen to him?" I raised my brows as I watched him casually move closer each time he spoke, as he had each time he had come. "Finn, I suggest you back up."

"Are you going to kill me?" he asked and took another step. Milo growled.

"He may," I answered and motioned at Milo.

"No, I don't think he will," Finn answered and took a few more steps forward. "He, like me, hears you at night, screaming. We all do. You may have stopped running through the damn forest at all hours of the night or starting fires the rest of us have to put out, but we all hear you, and we all come."

"I didn't ask you to," I answered. "I don't need you to come."

"I can smell your unshed tears." He took another step.

I stood. My hands curled into fists. "Don't."

"Or what, Perdi? You'll hurt me because I care? You'll end my life because I've come too close to you? You are *not* that person. You left that person in Whitwick. I carried a broken Crow back from hell."

"You have a short memory, Finn. I've killed for a lot less. I've killed simply because I can."

"No. You've killed to save your life and those you love."

"Love has done more damage to my soul than hate ever has." I laughed. "But it wasn't enough."

Finn stood at the bottom of the stairs and met my eyes. "It'll never be enough, little Crow."

I lunged off the stairs and clocked him in the jaw. "Don't call me that. Don't *ever* fucking call me that."

"Have I touched a sore spot, 'little Crow'?" Finn rotated his shoulders. I swung, and he leaned back. The heat from his skin kissed my knuckles as my fist passed by. "Oh, please. You don't have what it takes to hurt me. Not even the witches did, and you don't have the stomach to do worse than those hags. If I can sleep through their torture, you, little Crow, will be a walk in the park on a sunny day."

"Fuck you," I screamed and swung again, and he blocked me with ease.

"Fight or fuck, either way, you'll get what you need from me today," he said. They were the exact words he had said to me in his cave when we were hunting our enemies, both wearing masks of hate. But I wasn't wearing one today. I was angry and hurt and sick of the chaos. "It's okay, Perdi. I can take it."

"And I can't take another day of this shit," I answered.

"Yes, you can. Like me, you were born to suffer, and each time it'll feel like you want it to be the last. But you'll keep getting back up, you'll keep coming when innocents need you and you'll keep smashing your soul apart like glass. You may limp on and off that field, but you'll keep showing up," Finn said. "Your enemies will take everything from you, but they can never take who you are, who your soul demands you to be." Finn pushed me from his front. "You are the last Crow, but you're not the first. You're not unique in your suffering. You're not that special. None of us are. If you give up, those who did this to countless Crows before you will win. Those who died on our soil, broken Crows, died for nothing."

Finn motioned with his hand for me to try again. His smile irritated me like a rash. I swung again and connected with his jaw. His return jab came close, but I wasn't as slow as I once was. He taunted me until I lost control. Until I screamed my rage into his face. He, like Zephyr, brought me to the edge until all that came out was pain. And, as angry as I was, it felt good to let it out. When I brought him to the ground, my leg hooked behind his, I held him down with sheer will. I knew, if he wanted, I'd be out cold and wouldn't wake up until dinner. But he stayed under me and made me fight to remain on top. I swung, and he blocked. He grabbed my wrists, and I screamed until my voice finally cracked.

"Cry, little Crow. Let that water flow before you fucking drown in it." He pushed a blade into my hand. "Do it. It's what you want. To kill every Fae. To wipe us off the earth. I can feel it in your soul. I can taste it coat my tongue. The desire you have is thick enough to make a meal of. I've been there. I've wanted the death of everyone who crossed my path. To drink down the sweetness that could only come from the end of those I've hated, those who have hurt me beyond repair. I know exactly how it feels. If my death stops your pain, I give myself willingly. If my death means you'll live, take my life. I would rather die than watch you slowly fade." He positioned the blade over his heart and pulled it toward his body. I had to pull back, or I'd have pierced his heart and killed him. "Do it!" he screamed in my face with the same force I had used.

"No," I whispered. "That's not what I want."

"Kill me now, Perdi, because this doesn't end, and I can't watch it. What you feel doesn't ever end. Every day is this. You can't stop feeling just because you don't like it. Nothing you do, save death, will end this existence. You're not mortal, but you're not just Fae. You're a Soul-Eater, aligned with the greatest forces in Elphame." His words rattled against my bones. "What the fuck did you expect was going to happen? Every time I turn around, you've added another power to your lineup, and you wonder why you are a target for mortals and Fae. Hell, you're sitting on top of one of the most powerful Aos Si to ever be born. The only reason Zephyr is my commander is because he is Finis, and I am something much darker, something so bloody terrifying that I need someone else to control me." I pulled back and landed hard on my back. Finn rolled onto me and held me down. "We opened the door that should never be opened and bled a world dry. With that power comes payment and responsibility. *Your* people, mortals, their fates will be decided, and you just sit here. You are the only one in this bloody world who gives a shit about them."

"No, I don't," I answered, and it hurt to say the words. "I want to, but I just don't care."

"Then kill them. Because what will come for them will be everything you're running from. If you don't kill them, Elphame will. And they will do it in your name because of what they have done to you. Is that what you want? For your nightmares to become a reality for thousands? Do you want me to go back and show them why I need a Soul-Eater to control me? Because I plan to. I have every intention of killing every last one of them, for miles and miles, for what they did to us. They took my friend's fucking wings while he screamed for his life. I heard him, Perdi. I heard him begging for someone to kill him, and they laughed. They laughed as he cried. Every single time I close my fucking eyes, I hear what they did to us all." His voice shifted from anger to grief at the memory of Carver losing his wings. "Is that what you want? For mortals to feel your nightmares? Because I do. We all do. I want them to suffer. I want them to scream like my friends did. I want them to beg like Carver did, and I will laugh as hard as they did. I want to open the door to the darkest part of my magick and let it roll out as far as it can reach. I want it to be so fucking terrifying that not a single one of them tries to harm us again. Is that what you want? Do you want to see what I do to those I hate? What I'll do to avenge what they've done to my friends and family? Because it'll cost me nothing. I'm already suffering."

"No," I sputtered softly, scared of my own voice.

"Then end them, now," he replied. "Before those, who, by some miracle, survived, are sitting in some forest, terrified, like you. Have you enjoyed this life so much that you'd wish it on a child? On a mother with a baby in her womb? A mass Taking... That is what is coming for them. Vengeance will be ours. Fae never let a debt go unpaid."

"No, I can't just kill them," I answered.

"We're all taught how to love, but no one teaches us how or when to stop." He lifted off me to his hands and toes. He leaned into my ear. "Would you like me to kill them for you? Say the word. Just a whisper, Perdi, and I'll go back for you. I will go and punish them, all of them, for you. No one has to know it was you who asked. Do you want me to go back? I will do that for you, and we won't ever have to talk about what happens there."

I frowned. "No."

"Then you don't want them dead bad enough," he answered. "You want your hurt to stop, and their death isn't going to fix that. But you're happy enough to sit here and let others decide if they should live or die. You're a coward."

I shoved him off me. "No, I'm not."

He knelt beside me. "You're running away from something that will never go away. You lack the courage to face your fears, to endure the life you asked for, however dangerous or unpleasant it can become. You're scared of making a decision. That, I believe, is the definition of being a coward."

"I did make choices when I was there. I choose to punish them. I sentenced other people to death. I took their pearls, Finn—not because I had to, but because I hated them so much that I wanted them to suffer forever."

"And the pain of those choices isn't going to go away when you hide from it. How do you expect to heal, tucked away inside an old life you'll never have again?" he asked. "You either confront it or learn to live with it."

"I don't want to confront it." I finally admitted my truth to him. "I don't want to know how far-reaching my choices were when I chose to fight back. I don't want to know who else died or how they died. I don't need to know if Fae went to Whitwick once the Gate opened back up and killed children in the streets when we left. I don't want any new memories. The ones I have are bad enough."

"They didn't, if that helps. Those you said lived are still alive. The Fae left the moment all our people were across the Gate. The Aos Si scouted the mortal realm for miles and returned with a few stray Fae still alive. The Sluagh carried the fallen home, and all Fae followed," he answered.

One of the knots sitting in my stomach relaxed to the answer. "I'm glad all of our people, dead or alive, came home."

"Perdi, if your decisions reached farther than you can imagine, what then? Are you going to fix it? Will you make sure it doesn't happen again or let it continue to play out? Are you going to stop the deaths or allow more to go to their graves that should have been marked with your name the day you were Taken? And if Fae kill your people indiscriminately, what the hell are you going to do about it? You're either too mortal to be taken seriously here and are nothing more than a doormat, or you're Fae enough for everyone to listen when you speak. Both come at a cost."

"I'm scared of what I'll do if I go to Blood and Bones and hear the answers to my questions," I answered.

"There's only one place you can confront all that," Finn replied. "Go to the meeting and point blank ask them. Ask what their plans are, and ask about those they plan to kill next. They won't be able to lie to you, not in Blood and Bones. You can ask and leave, even if you don't add to the conversation."

"And if they tell me truths I don't want to hear? What happens if they tell me they're going to invade the mortal world and kill them all?"

"At least they'll all be in one room," he answered. "It'll be easier to kill them all if they're together. Say the word, and the rest of us will follow you back into hell.

Worry not, little Crow. The Aos Si don't mind the flames. We can outrun the consequences long enough for Solas and Zephyr to calm down. Together, we can hide for however long it takes for them to settle down. They'd probably get over it in a few decades, but that's a few decades of vacation to us. It's a win-win. We solve your problem, and we get a holiday from this shit."

"Speaking of... Solas and Zephyr would stop me," I replied.

"No, we wouldn't. We were built for war, little Crow." Solas stepped out of the house with a small towel in his hand. "Don't you ever wash the dishes?"

Both Finn and I jumped to our feet. Finn stepped back. "I was just leaving, sir."

"The hell you were, Finn." Solas jumped off the stairs. "Waging war inside Blood and Bones, killing every royal and High-Fae in Elphame? That's your solution?"

Finn shrugged. "It was merely a suggestion. Perhaps not one of my better ideas, I admit, but one I favor."

"You sound like Zephyr whenever there's a problem," Solas answered.

"Give me death or give me war. The rest is just a dance building up to the bloody cleanup." Finn grinned ear to ear, cocky as ever.

I smiled. "I tried to tell you to leave, Finn."

He leaned in. "You could have told me Solas was here. I wouldn't have suggested we killed all of them. Maybe a couple to prove a point, but not all."

"He won't leave, either," I answered. "He comes every day."

"I'll just be going now." Finn backed away. "See you next week, little Crow."

"No, you won't," I answered.

"Yes. I will." He walked through the front gate and was gone.

Solas turned back to the house. "Lunch is ready."

I rolled my eyes and followed him inside.

Chapter Twelve

Solas had cleaned while Finn and I argued. Guilt pricked my heart at the sight of Solas. Despite the dreams that haunted me, Solas was a good man with a kind soul. He moved around my father's kitchen with a smile, even though he must have known what was coming. Every other time, it ended with me losing my temper or crying until my flames threatened to burn my childhood home to ash.

"Solas, you don't have to do this."

"I know." He pulled out a chair for me. "I do it because I love you, not because I have to."

"Isn't it hard being here with me and my anger?" I asked.

"Yes, very much so. But love isn't about only being with someone when it's easy. Love means we show up for the good and the bad." He took a seat across from me. "Potatoes?"

I frowned. "No, I'm good, thanks."

"Two scoops, coming right up," he answered with a wink, and I smiled.

I pushed my food around my plate while Solas talked about his day. It was like every other meal I had ever shared with him since my return from Whitwick. He always came, cleaned from my temper, cooked my favorite foods and talked about his day as if the world around me wasn't on fire. On nights when all I could do was scream at him, he would nod, agree and correct the parts I got wrong. Each layer of memory he helped scab back over. There were some things I still wasn't brave enough to ask about. But he was still there when I couldn't contain my rage. And he stayed when the fire threatened to burn us both.

"What's on your mind this afternoon?" he asked.

"What Finn said, that I had to confront things or learn to live with them," I answered.

"You're not to type to just live with something, Perdi. But you'll do it in your own time. Don't let him pressure you into doing something you're not ready for." Solas put his fork down and clasped his hands under his chin. He was preparing for me to lose my temper. I watched his shoulders tense, and he grounded himself in preparation. I felt guilty. Every time he came, I had something new to be angry about. It felt like every wound I had healed, I had to start over on. Yet, he still came back every day. He answered my questions and still loved me in all my madness.

"I appreciate that you come here, Solas. But it hurts at the same time."

"That, I would agree on," he replied. "But healing never feels good. At least, for me, it never has. It always feels worse experiencing it a second time around. Don't be so hard on yourself. You're going at a pace your soul is comfortable with. You've been through lifetimes of pain and grief in a short amount of time. It's okay to do what you must, to feel whole again."

"Solas, what did Zephyr do with all the pearls I gave him?" I finally asked the question that had weighed heavily since returning from Whitwick. I ate their souls for the energy but bound their pearls with hate.

"He doesn't speak to me of his souls, but from what Nix has said, Zephyr released most of them and kept only the witches, Mages and those who harmed your father. Why do you ask? Do you feel bad for those who stood against you?"

I shrugged. "I don't really know. I don't feel bad for those who took me. I feel like I should, but I don't. I know mortals were scared, but what they did to me wasn't done out of fear. It was done through hatred. I guess I just wanted to know what Zephyr did to clean up my mess."

"Why don't you talk to him and ask?"

"He doesn't come around much anymore," I replied. "I can feel him, but I don't see him often."

"He's always close by. He doesn't want to push you. He sees you making progress each day and doesn't want to derail that by needling you or showing you your truth faster than your soul can handle. What happened for you to leave Whitwick is an awful burden for you to carry. Finn has told us of the journey, as have the other survivors. Zephyr has been there. He remembers what it feels like to unleash all a Soul-Eater is just to survive. When you're ready, he will come. Until then, he's happy to watch you heal, feel your pearl slowly repair and wait for your call."

I put my fork down and swallowed the lump in the back of my throat. "The decisions I've made…" I raised my hand to stop him from opening his mouth. "Not *we*. The decisions *I* made on my own haunt me. I appreciate, more than I could ever say, your willingness to carry the blame with me. But the decisions that were mine to make are my responsibility to own. I closed the Gate, Solene destroyed it and I carried on as if none of it would bite me in the ass. It did. I killed to leave the Golden Court and many times again to survive long enough to close the Gate. I killed your sister for the Gate. I killed an island of people because of that Gate. It doesn't matter to me that someone else chose to hunt the Satyr and forced them to retaliate. It only matters that my only recourse was to kill them. Mortals were put in the same position. They took me and tortured us because they feared all Fae, including me. And the only way to stop it was more death. I know the path I chose to walk would mean that I'd suffer, but I'm so sick and tired of people dying for me and at my hand. Death can't be the only way for me to live." It felt good to say the words out loud, as ashamed as I was of the truth. "I'm so tired of that fucking Gate. It always comes back to that Gate."

"Hundreds of years, Perdi, it's always been about that Gate," he replied. "It has been the center of so much pain, lives lost, futures gone."

"My entire life has been about the Gate and the fears of Elphame, the Fae, the cursed life of becoming a Crow. And now, I'm all raw from it again. It's like the healing I had done is gone. It feels like the first day that I woke up in the manor," I replied. "I wasn't brave enough before to ask questions. I was as scared then as I am now to know the truth. But I'll never heal if I don't ask those questions." I closed my eyes and shivered. Fear was a weird emotion. I either froze under its touch, raged to cure it or bolted. Today, though, I'd force myself to stay seated and talk it out. "Growing up, as a mortal, we were told that when Fae came to Whitwick with the fog, being so close to Fae made us do horrible things to each other."

"This is true," he replied.

"My question, Solas, the one that won't stop digging to get out, is, how much of that is actually true?" I asked.

"It is true, but it's also not true. It depends on who is wielding the magick. When Fae entered Whitwick, only the worst of Elphame went for the Taking. Most had no choice but to go. They were forced. Some, however, enjoyed the terror, enjoyed causing chaos. Elphame sent its horrors on purpose. Standing that close to power that dark, bled terror onto everyone else around them, whether on purpose or not. Kings sent their worst, their nightmares, and enjoyed the fear they caused because, for some Fae, mortals were beneath them. But even if Fae had been calm when they went through the Gate, our energy and the very fear we evoke with our coming would cause countless people to go mad. You've seen what we do to each other, the chaos we cause within our own lands. Mortals stood little chance."

"I guess, more than that question, I want to know what my friends did when they came. I want to know if those I care about killed people for sport. On the day of my Taking, I have memories of Fae killing children in the streets. I remember Faolan in my living room, with fresh blood under his nails, and I wonder what the hell he was doing before he got to me to be bloodied? Did he kill one of the townspeople before he got to my house?"

"No. Faolan has never participated in the horrors unleashed upon mortals. He only ever came to protect you. As much as it pains me to defend him, especially when it comes to you and your Taking, he never allowed himself to get caught up in terrorizing your people, as so many others did. The day you were Taken, I watched you run home with Faolan close behind you. When he saw me in front of your house, he broke my nose. He jumped me and punched me four times. It was a bloody mess. It's why I was already bloody when I got to you. It was the only time he's ever struck me, and the only time I'd have let him live for it."

I smiled and couldn't help but laugh. "You kind of deserved it."

"And much more, Perdi. I was there to Take you away from your home. I stole you into the very land you now suffer for. Whether you feel like he was your traitor or not, he hated me for it, almost as much as I hated myself. He made sure I felt it before I got to you."

"The day you came for me, I saw you, on the street, in front of my house. I heard you calling my name," I replied and winced at the memory. "And when you came to Whitwick after I was Taken by the witches, I could hear you calling my name again, and it brought me right back to the first time I had heard it, back to the day I had become a Crow."

"I know. I could feel your fear. I could smell your tears, and they reminded me of what I had felt the day I stole you from Whitwick. Everything about that day was exactly like the day of your Taking, from the fog to the Fae in the streets to the screams of terror. It's why I stepped back and didn't reach for you," he replied. "I remember that day clearly. The day you were Taken as a Crow, I saw you in the front window watching me. I remember standing on your front walk and laughing."

"Laughing?" I asked.

"Not the kind of laughter you think. More frustration. I stood in front of the one house I never wanted to come to and was forced to do the one thing I couldn't stop. You were fated to become a Crow, yet I thought I'd be able to save you from this. For all this power I had, all the fear others had of me, I couldn't stop the one thing I didn't want to do."

"I saw you kill children in the street in front of my house," I blurted out. "Why would you do that?"

"No, Perdi. That never has happened. I swear to any oath. I've never done that," he answered. "You were marked for the Taking, which attracted every Fae to your home. Those who came, Fae who wanted into your house to torment you before you were Taken, I killed them in the streets. But I've never harmed a mortal during the Taking. Oh, I threatened, but I never did."

"Why did you threaten to hurt mortals?"

"Crows, Perdi," he corrected. "I wanted to speed them along. The sooner they agreed to leave, the sooner Elphame would be sucked back through the Gate. The longer Fae remained in the mortal realm, the more suffering that came. But, if I could scare them into leaving, their people wouldn't suffer in their place. It was harsh and cruel, but it would have been so much worse had I not."

"But I remember…" I groaned in frustration. "When I was Taken, the *first* time, it sounds funny to say that out loud. Bits and pieces I didn't remember until now are coming back. When the witches took me, I was shown memories. I don't know if they are real, and I'm scared to hear the truth."

"It's okay, little Crow." Solas' face softened. "Is this why you've been hiding out here? Your memories?"

"I came here because I needed to sort out my head without Elphame's constant picking at my soul like vultures. Elphame doesn't stop spitting out chaos just because I'm wounded. I needed to be away from everything, or I couldn't figure anything out on my own," I answered. "But I remember it differently now. Even the parts I know aren't real, hurt as if they were. It's hard to explain. The parts I know are a lie feel like the truth, no matter what my mind tells my soul."

"You have my pearl. Why not look and see what I know?" he asked. "You will see what happened, what I remember, what I did and didn't do."

"I'm not like Zephyr. I can't read pearls unless I grab onto them and concentrate. But right now, I can't see beyond what I feel and fear. I think I'm too scared to see the truth just yet."

"I remember that day, Perdi. I remember it as crystal clear as yesterday. The problem is, for the most part, you remember it exactly the same way I do. The only real difference is the emotions behind the memories. I remember stepping onto mortal soil and feeling the rush of excitement…the screaming and terror. For those of us who were born and bred for war, it is everything to us, and we get a little confused at first. It took several minutes of standing there, on the other side of the Gate, to calm myself. The urge to join in is incredible. The impulse to become a monster that stalks the night is everything I have fought against. But for those first few minutes, it reminded me of stepping foot onto the battlefield."

"The Taking wasn't war, Solas. It was death," I countered. "Death and fear."

"And any war fought against me is not war, Perdi. It is only death and fear." He answered with a truth I had seen for myself. "But going into Whitwick, against my will, made me hate—not mortals, but why I had to go. I knew about you and my purpose, but I really wanted to dislike you initially. I was scared you weren't the one, and we all would keep suffering, both your people and mine. I was scared I'd have to do it again and again. It killed parts of me every time I came, and the Crow died. It is a lot to keep asking of myself. I cursed myself for the oath between Aoife and me. I gave my word to your greatest of grandmothers, that I'd find you and save you—that together, we'd end the Taking of Crows. So, I suffered for you and didn't even know you. My people died for you, and I hadn't even met you. Zephyr, the fool, was locked in a dungeon for you. Everything and everyone I loved was balancing on me being a monster, and I hated it. It was so hard to be calm when I saw you. Even though I knew none of it was your fault, I stood in front of your house and laughed at where I was. The Crow who would end it all was also the Crow who I didn't want to Take. I didn't want to Take any of you. It was all too much.

"Then I saw you with Faolan. For the briefest of moments, I thought I had done it all for nothing. I didn't think I'd ever be able to convince you that I wasn't your enemy. I remember being on the boat, right after we took you, and I wanted to hate you so badly. It shook me to my core. If I hated you, I thought it would be easier to watch you be another Crow to die. Hate and anger are much easier to deal with than any other emotion here in Elphame."

"It's the same no matter where you are," I added. "There's little room for anything else unless you're willing to kill for it."

"Ain't that the truth." He frowned at the reality we all knew a little too well. "On the boat, I wanted to toss you over the edge and be done with it all. The appeal of going back to the Dark Court and saying 'screw it' was strong, no matter the consequences. War had to be better than suffering over and over again. Nix yelled at me for hours, and all I could think of was getting your blood and vomit off my hands from carrying you. I didn't want to touch you. I just wanted it to end. For once, just let it be over. Nix, on the other hand, was willing to go to war against me to save you."

"I remember, now, being in the boat and you telling Nix that if I didn't make it, I wasn't the one," I answered.

He nodded. "I said a lot of things on that boat, Perdi. But I also fed you power and allowed the others to do the same, to keep your heart going. I was caught somewhere between love and hate. I hated who I was, hated who I had become and truly blamed you and your line for it. But when we docked, and you were willing to fight me, that's when I knew, it wasn't you who I hated. It was myself. The moment you ran and I chased you, the Sluagh were coming for you."

"I remember them," I replied. "They were a terrifying introduction to the beasts of Elphame."

"They weren't coming to kill you, Perdi. They were coming to help you," he answered. "They felt a Finis come through the Gate. Both the Finis and Sluagh are not fully of Elphame, and they heard the call of another like them, apart from this world. The moment you stepped on Elphame soil, you woke every Sluagh in

Elphame. When you ran, your fear called to the Sluagh. That was the first day the dragons came out of hiding and brought word to the wee folks, the last Crow had finally come. I knew, as they were circling above us, you were the one that would help me stop the Taking of Crow, stop Solene calling them to their doom and would become the last Crow. Everyone was prepared for your coming…everyone but me."

"That makes one of us," I replied. "I didn't have the same faith in myself as you."

"I would disagree. You faced off against me on more than one occasion. Where others cowered, you stood firm. You took on the entire Golden Court to save lives, Perdi. You did that, no one else. You, a gnome, a fairy and a once-slave, ended the reign of a mad king and rescued those deemed worthless. You made it from one end of Elphame to the other as a hunted Crow. You did the impossible, over and over. If that's not faith, I don't know what is," he said with a smile. "Even though we ended the Taking and I tell myself it was worth becoming a monster, I still remember the day I came for you and my heart breaks every time. Each time you've come home from Whitwick, I cringe at the smell you carry on your skin. I have hated the very smell of the place and the memories it evokes. It turns my stomach whenever I catch the scent in the air. It brings me back to who I had to be, and I hate it. I could only imagine what you must feel like, to be Taken into this world, then Taken again, only to hate yourself for what you've had to do to survive it all. I've hated myself for the same reasons."

"I feel exactly like I had when I was finally free from the Golden Court. Those weeks I spent trying to put myself back together? It feels the same today as it did then. I feel raw, and I don't know where I belong. I'm glad the Taking is over, but I miss who I was before I was named a Crow. I miss my dad. I miss everything Elphame took from me. It still feels brand new, even though it isn't."

"And you're free to be where you need to be until it stops being raw. You're free to live as you'd like," Solas answered. "If that means you go back to the mortal world to get back what was taken from you, then that is where you need to go. You're not in a prison. You're free to live whatever life you want and need. My love for you doesn't come with ownership."

"I don't belong there. It hurts to admit it, but I never want to go back. I have no reason to and don't want anyone to ever ask me to stick my head out of the other side of that Gate. I've given them enough of myself. They don't get any more from me. I may be raw, but I haven't forgotten what they did to me and what I know they'd do to me again if they could," I answered. "I don't want them all to die, but they aren't my home. *This* is my home. *You* are my home. It may just take more time for me to get there again. I'm sorry, Solas. I'm really trying. It might look like I'm not and that I'm content with sitting here and wallowing in self-pity, but I'm trying to fix myself the best I can."

He stood and walked to my side. From his knees, he reached forward, slowly, with his hand. "Read it all, Perdi. There are no walls, no secrets. If you can't read my pearl inside you, you can dig your way through my mind. I won't stop you. I won't lie to you. You need to see and feel the truth in all its sharp bits. More than that, you need to know that you are not alone."

I shook my head. "What happens if I can't handle it?"

"Then I die while you rage inside my soul, I suppose," he answered with a wink.

"You don't want that, Solas." I shivered at the memory of what I had done to Faolan's mind when I was desperate enough to leave him a husk of a man for the truth.

"No, I don't, but I don't want this, either." He closed his eyes and waited for me to come as the force he knew I could be. "I will come back every day until I die, if that is what it takes. I don't care where I lay my head as long as it is near you. But this, you alone? I can't do that part. I can't watch you cry and not hold you. I can't stand on the edge of your life and watch as you suffer alone. I love you. Look inside my soul, Perdi. All I have is yours to see. And any parts that are still missing, we will find whoever has that information, and I'll hold them down for you."

I reached for his hand with a smile. He didn't flinch or pull back. He looked up and waited. Nothing in his eyes said he feared what I'd do or see. He was willing to relive every thought, memory and deed, good or bad. And as I held his warm hand, my Malice didn't budge. She, like my soul, knew there was nothing to read that I didn't already know or hold in his pearl. There were a million reasons for a person to fear Solas, to step back when he entered the room. But I would never feel those reasons. I would never need to step back or hide from him. He would protect me until his last day, when fate would have to fight a nightmare for his dying breath. There was nothing left to prove, so I left his memories where they belonged.

"I have the answers I need," I finally said.

"You don't believe me?" He drew back, but I grabbed his hand and held it a little tighter.

"I do. I don't need to flex my Malice to hear your soul or know your truth. When I came back, I was scared to know what was real. I was scared to ask the questions, not just of you but of myself. I remember who I had to become, and facing those dark corners of my soul, tore me apart. As angry at the world as I've been, you're not one of the reasons I'm angry," I replied. "I didn't want to hurt you by questioning you. But I had to know if you were hiding the truth from me—the truth of who I am and who my friends are. And I don't need to read your soul to know what really matters. The rest will heal, and I know I won't have to do the hard parts alone. I know I'll never have to face the horrors of this world on my own. What I've done eats me up inside. But this, us, you, doesn't hurt. I love you and have never stopped."

"And I love you." He pulled me from the chair into his lap. "You won't always like everything you will see inside me, but I swore to you that I'd never hide again. All my monstrous bits are yours."

"I don't think you'd like what you'd see if you took a peek into my soul, either."

"I will never see something I can't handle. If anything, I'll see someone who needs to be loved a little harder." He kissed my forehead and pulled me tight against his body. And although we sat inside my childhood home, it was tucked in his arms where I felt most at home. "I have never doubted your resolve, little Crow—or your capacity to love. But I also have never doubted you would do what is right, regardless of how much of your soul you'll break off. Trust that I'll always be here to put you back together."

"I didn't leave you, Solas. But I couldn't be your queen, a Crow and myself, all at once. I had to be just me, selfishly me, and heal that part before I could look at the rest."

"I've only ever wanted you, Perdi. Just you. Nothing more or less than what you wanted to give."

"Let's go home," I whispered into his mouth.

Solas picked me up and carried me home, wrapped in his darkness, with Milo in the sky above us and Zephyr trailing behind. I felt his pearl deep inside sigh in relief. I was home, really home—and I would be okay.

Chapter Thirteen

I stepped into the manor and breathed my first calming breath since leaving Elphame as a Crow for the mortal world. Any broken pieces still left in my soul began to patch up as soon as I smelled the lavender and mint. I could feel the Aos Si close by, smell Milo's spicy musk as he landed in the backyard and feel the shadows roaming the halls. It was exactly as it had been the last time I was home, from the ebb and flow to the scent and feel of my home against my soul.

"Is she okay?" Nix's voice came from the hall. "Do you think I should make her apple pies or turnovers? Maybe you could bring them to her for a snack later…or maybe not. The memory of her mother may bother her right now… Perdi?" Nix froze, then smiled as soon as he saw me. "Perdi, you're home."

I smiled as he climbed up my leg to my shoulder. "Yes, I'm home."

"I'll set the table for coffee and cakes," Solas said as he moved past me. "Oisin and Faolan are outside, telling Zephyr and Finn that they felt you leave your father's house with Milo."

"You might as well invite them all in. Afternoon tea is better had with family and friends. I'm going to shower and change," I called back and walked with Nix to my bedroom.

"Did you know that Orrian is pregnant?" Nix asked and ignored the wounds I had come home with. He carried on as if I had been here yesterday and the day before.

"What? Since when?" I asked, kicking off my boots and pants. Nix followed me into my bathroom.

"Apparently, that's why she's been going hog wild over her fruit trees and her gardens. She was preparing for her birthing cycle." Nix jumped onto the far shelf in the shower while I scrubbed off the smell of pity and sadness with the soap Nix had made himself. The scent of rosemary, lavender and mint filled the room. It smelled like the Dark Courts, like home.

"Who is the father?" I asked.

"Carver!" Nix yelled over the roar of the shower. "I didn't even know they were a couple. Did he say anything to you about it?"

I shook my head. "No, but it makes sense. I saw them dancing together at my birthday party. And while we were on the run, he had mentioned he was thankful Orrian hadn't come through the Gate."

"She has seven of those little suckers in her oven."

"Seven? Holy hell. Is that normal for her people?" I asked.

"It's her first batch. She'll probably have several more if the Gods bless them. The next few will probably result in a dozen each time."

"Dear God, could you imagine that many babies at once?"

"And they say gnomes breed like crazy? We only have two or three at once," he replied. "Don't even get me started on pixies. They shoot them out faster than clouds can make rain."

I laughed at his humor. I missed how easily Nix could turn a moment into something worth smiling over. I turned off the water and dried off. "What are Orrian's customs? Do I send her a gift?"

"Whatever you do, do not send her a fruit tree. She'll take it as you don't think she can provide food for her newlings. You could offer to ward a room for her? When her children are born, they are at risk for a year after, as is her court. If she had a room of protection against those who wished them harm, she'd be able to defend her territory. I could help find some nice stones to spell and go into her den to place them for you? You'd trash the place with your big feet."

"That's a great idea, Nix," I answered. I pulled on fresh clothes that fit me much better than my old clothes at my father's house and twisted my hair into a braid. "Shall we?"

"I'm glad you're home, Perdi," Nix answered and jumped from the bed to my shoulder. "Solas is a bore without you around. If I hear another story about you, or how you do something cute, how you smell, what you're thinking of or how you like things done a certain way, I'll vomit. Do you know how many bloody potatoes he made the rest of us eat?"

I paused at the door, then stepped back to my bed. I scooted Nix from my shoulder as I sat. "Nix…thank you."

He patted my hand. "Always and forever."

I clasped his small hand and fought against the urge to cry. "The only good thing about reliving my Taking is that I remembered you and everything you did to make sure I lived through it. I wouldn't have made it without you. You fought tooth and nail for me to get here. You've never once stopped helping me or asked for anything in return. I love you more than life. I love you for who you are. I love all the parts, including those you feel shame for. I love how utterly ruthless you are and that you come into my bedroom every night to kiss my nose. You don't think I know you do it, but I hear you tell me you love me every night. And while I was at my dad's, I still felt you come, still heard the words, and I love you for always being the softer side of Elphame."

"It's what you do for your family. You love all their brokenness pieces until they can get back up and face another day," he replied. "I'll go into hell for you."

"And I would do the same for you," I replied. "Where are your sister and her children?"

"Right now, they're close by. My nephew, Rex, is working with Aeden and Jayde. He's healing from the mortal world. But they will leave for the Hallows in a couple of weeks once Rex stops having nightmares."

I swallowed a rock in my throat. "Nix, I gift you my father's home, the garden and the land. Bring your family home, closer to us. I would feel better if we kept our family closer."

"I'm happy here with you, Perdi." He shook his head. "I don't want to leave here."

"Then don't," I replied. "This is my home, with Solas. My dad's house is empty, and it will remain as such. Your family is welcome to go to live there for as long as you'd like. The house and land are yours, but your home will always be with me."

"But I am a courtless gnome. When my line was killed by Solene, my title died with them. I cannot own land here."

I opened my bedside table and removed a rolled-up parchment, sealed with the Dark Court emblem...a black wax Sluagh. "I didn't have the chance to give this to you before I was Taken. I was planning a banquet, honoring those most loyal to our court, where I was going to gift this to you, but war got in the way, as it does."

He broke the seal and unrolled the paper. I watched his eyes dart across the page and his mouth drop open as he read it. His hands began to shake as he reread it. "I am restored? The Seers have given me back my title?"

I nodded. "It was taken by Solene when she killed your family. What she took from you has been gifted back, with interest. Lily, at Blood and Bones, has your first payment in the form of gold. Solas has decreed that Solene's war chest is transferred to those who suffered from Solene's crimes. This is for you, for your loyalty to Solas and to me."

He shook his head and read the paper out loud. "Sir Nix Lubdan, of the Ulster Territory, descendant of King Lubdan, Royal Fae of the Dark Courts."

"That certainly has a nice ring to it, Sir Nix." I smiled and bowed my head.

"I don't even know what to say." His face flushed.

"Say you'll hang your family crest on the home you've shared with me for most of my life," I answered.

"But I won't have to leave here, right?"

"No, your home is with me. But your family? Their home is close to you."

He nodded. "This will tickle my sister and her children. They'll have titles to grow into, land, a garden and futures. They will have a home that is not borrowed. A gnome with their own garden is a greater gift than any title. This, Perdi, is a gift beyond measure."

"As is your friendship," I replied.

Nix climbed back onto my shoulder and nudged me with his boot. "Onward, donkey. This royal is hungry."

I threatened to push him off the next time he kicked me into gear, and we headed for the dining room, following the sounds of laughter and the mixed smells of Elphame coming together under one roof, yet again.

"Nix," Finn called out to him, "I saved you a peanut butter cookie. Zephyr swallowed down the entire plate."

Nix jumped to the arm of his chair and thumbed his nose in the air. "That is Sir Nix, thank you, you bloody peasant."

"You told him, I see." Solas grinned.

"It's going straight to his head," I answered. "Did you know about Orrian?" I asked him as I took a seat. I motioned to my stomach and puffed out my checks.

Solas nodded with a grin. "We suspected Orrian was close to her lush years. She has a bloody orchard out there." I stared at him quizzically. "Her fertile years. For a fairy, they refer to it as lush years, where her womb is…"

"I get it," I answered, and he sighed in relief for not having to explain the reproductive workings of a fairy. "The great and honorable Sir Nix and I are gifting her a warded room to protect her young, so she can still defend her territory without worrying her children are at risk."

Around pieces of cookie, Nix spoke, little crumbles falling to the table. "And what will the Dark King be getting her? You're not signing your name on our card. You need to come up with your own idea."

"A fruit tree?" he asked, and the room gasped. "Or not. I don't know. Jewels and gold? She likes shiny things."

Zephyr passed me a cup of tea and a small plate of cookies in the shape of a Crow. "I will be hand-crafting swords for her young and inviting her first-born son to train with the Aos Si." He glanced at Solas. "Top that, oh great king of ours."

"There's this little island off the coast of Blood and Bones. It falls within the water territory of the Dark Courts," Solas teased. "I double-checked the maps. It already has a house and a garden. I think Orrian would love it."

Zephyr snickered. "Getting desperate, are you?"

"I heard about Orrian from Oberon," Oisin chimed in. "I've begun to craft small stone charms for her young in the shape of snowflakes. They will always find friends in the Winter Court."

"Bloody hell, how are you all so ready?" Finn asked. "I only just heard about Orrian this morning."

"Welcome to the club," Solas answered.

"You're on your own, Solas," Finn countered. "I already dropped off a row of rocking beds. I carved them on my way over. As if I'd get caught with my pants down."

"Yes, we'd hate for your pants to be down in front of Perdi again," Zephyr snarled, and the rest of us laughed, except for Finn, who blushed.

"How are you doing?" Faolan asked while Solas was teased by both Finn and Zephyr.

"The road home can be long and bumpy, but I made it," I replied. "Thank you for coming to check on me. One night, when it was particularly bad, I could smell Christmas in the air and knew you were close by."

"Oh, that wasn't on purpose," he laughed. "The night you're so fond of, your winged beast had both Oisin, and I pinned down in the backyard. Leave it to you to have a thunder of dragons. They set my shirt on fire. It was probably my fear that you smelled."

"Milo isn't much of a people person," I countered.

"Neither are you," Finn pointed out. "It's a good match."

"Speak for yourself, Faolan. I had a great time. Being chased by a Sluagh was the highlight of my week," Oisin added. "More than the thrill of the life-and-death experience of visiting you, I like that the dragons are swarming again. They've been in and out of Oberon's caves. They don't seem to mind the feeling of dread. It's good luck to see them in your court. It means they see you as a friend, a place of peace and safety. Oberon is absolutely tickled to have them in his caves."

"I wouldn't say I'm a place of peace or safety," I replied.

Oisin grinned. "You may be war, but your reasons are noble enough to follow you into hell."

The rest of the evening melted away into laughter, teasing and remembering why we always found our way back home. We didn't pick at the scabs that brought us crawling through the front door, but we didn't ignore the wounds not yet healed. Slowly, the house emptied. Finn and Zephyr went to the caves with Milo, Nix to his family to share his good news and the

Winter Court back to where frost made me smile and snow melted my bad dreams.

I rolled into the arms of the man who made everything right in the world and breathed him in. "I love you more than words can say."

"I feel it, Perdi." He lifted my chin and placed his hot lips against mine. "I'll eat your nightmares until the day I die."

"When that day comes, I'll eat the world for taking you."

"You say the sweetest things to me," he whispered and pushed me onto my back. "But now is not the time for sweet nothings. Hold on tight. I've got moves you've never seen."

As he had before, he invited me into his darkness. It was a place that terrified all but me. Little wisps of inky night leaked from his fingertips as he cupped my face for a kiss. I opened my soul to him, allowing his darkness to move between us. No words could describe the passion and love that swirled like flames between us. Moments stretched impossibly long...seconds to minutes to hours. In what took a blink of an eye, it felt like we had lost the very idea of time. The world was gone, and everything that tethered us down faded. He pushed his darkness into my soul, and I melted under him. It was exquisite in all its layers.

When we floated back down to reality, it took several minutes for me to utter a single word. "Water."

Solas inched his way to the edge of the bed and dragged a bottle of water to my side. "It's too heavy to lift."

I huffed a laugh. "My arms don't want to work."

"Neither do mine."

Slowly, we untangled our bodies just enough to each drink a bottle of water. Solas stayed half-curled over my lower body. I was happy in whatever position I was in, as long as it was beside him. The calm slowly returned, and I sunk into it. There weren't many moments like this in Elphame, and I would love every second gifted to me. The feel of his heart against me had settled my soul in ways nothing else could.

"You're such a big talker," I finally said. "I've seen those moves before."

Solas jerked and sat up with a grin. "Oh, have you now?"

I jumped from the bed and wiggled my eyebrows. Solas tracked my movement at the foot of the bed and landed behind me before I could close the bathroom door. The entire house, if not the court, heard me scream and him laugh as he tugged me into the shower. We took turns washing each other, ignoring my new scars and kissing the old ones. Elphame had taught us many lessons the hard way, but it was Whitwick that left the deepest marks on us both. We had come close, many times, to losing each other, but none as close to me becoming a Crow of the mortal world.

We watched as dawn climbed from her slumber, tucked around each other. This was exactly where I wanted to be, where I *needed* to be. "I could live in this moment forever."

He pulled me as tight as he could. "As could I. But the world doesn't stop for us. *Sleep*, little Crow. Thrones don't care how tired we are."

"Stay with me until I wake up," I whispered through the push of his magick.

"Forever," he answered.

I dreamed of Zephyr as I slept, tucked safely in the arms of Solas. I don't remember why he had come while I slept, but I hadn't cried out in terror for the first time in a long time.

Chapter Fourteen

Solas landed in front of the bloodstained wall with me at his side. He didn't flinch at the sight of Blood and Bones, but I recoiled as much today as I always had. I shivered from head to toe. My nerves were not endless, and this place tested them to their limits. Solas was used to the pressure, but I felt like I would pop under it and add a new splash of blood on their walls. Each time I've come, it's never been for a good reason, and the last time I was here, I was ripped from my home and Taken into the land of mortals. This place was bound to leave a stain on my soul.

"You don't have to be here, Perdi." Solas called my mind out of my dark thoughts. "If this is too much, I can take you home. We can leave any time, and we go together. You are not alone today and not ever again. To hell with the others if they don't understand. You owe them nothing."

"I need a minute." I motioned to Finn, who was leaning casually against the wall to my right. There was nothing casual about Finn. That he was trying to look the part told me something was up.

"Zephyr is already here. I'll meet you inside. Take your time. The others can damn well wait for you." Solas kissed my temple and gave Finn a stern look. "Whatever the reason for your being here, try to keep her soul in one piece."

Finn pushed off the wall with a grin as Solas stepped behind it to meet with the others. "Good to see you're back to showering regularly, little Crow. You were starting to stink."

"I didn't get a chance to tell you last night. Thank you." I stepped forward and hugged him. "For coming, even when I asked you not to, even when I made it absolute hell to be near me."

He pulled back. "Taking your shit and abuse wasn't my idea."

"Zeph?" I asked.

He smiled at my use of Zephyr's nickname. "I drew the short stick with the Aos Si trainees. I was put on Crow cleanup duty. They didn't think you'd kill me as fast as the others. I kept telling them it was Solas we had to worry about, but they sent me anyway."

"Nice." I rolled my eyes.

"I'd have come, regardless. Coming to you healed me as much as it helped you," Finn answered and squeezed my hand. "You don't crawl out of hell with someone and leave them to heal the wounds on their own. Elphame is hard enough to survive on a good day. We shouldn't have to face it alone on a bad one."

"Thank you." My smile faded as soon as my attention went back to the wall of Blood and Bones. "I hate coming here. It's tainted. So many bad memories are attached to this place. It seems like every time I come back here, I leave with another reason to dislike this place."

"I'm glad I'm not going in. This place gives me the creeps. It feels like I have to force myself to stay while my soul is waiting for me at the border," he replied and rubbed the center of his chest, something I did when it felt like the world had grown too heavy for my shoulders. "The first time you came here, I almost didn't miss, on purpose. I was willing to shoot you down just so I could leave."

"You were the one that shot at me?" I asked.

"Be glad. I'm a better shot than the others." His soft laugh made me smile.

"Next time you shoot at me, I'll find you in your cave when you're sleeping," I answered. "You won't have a birthmark when I'm done."

"I look forward to the day you come." He grinned with promise. "Until then, I'll enjoy each day like it will be my last."

"Why aren't you coming inside? I thought your mom was a Seer?" I asked.

"That doesn't mean I ever want to come here. Not all of us are as happy with where we started out in this world. And with Solene here, none of us ever wanted to catch her eye. Now, she's left a stain on the place many of us can't forget. The memory of who she was still crawls across my brain and tells me to hide. Some scars don't heal, no matter how hard we try."

"Same with me. I know Solene is dead, but the fear she left behind? I can still feel it. It's like she's still here, waiting around the corner for me."

"There aren't many people in the world who I am truly happy are gone. But the day you killed her was one of my better days," he answered, and I agreed. I grieved for every death I had dealt out, except for hers. I was happy she was gone, and I've never lost a wink of sleep because of it. "Are you ready for this? Deciding the fate of an entire people at a table of those who will pay no cost for it?"

"No, I'm not. But it's not like there are many choices to pick from," I answered and watched a grin form that said he had been scheming. "I take it you have a different suggestion?"

He grinned. "We do."

"Who is this *we* you're referring to?" I asked.

"Aos Si trainees," he answered. "No one ever listens to us, but we usually have quicker solutions. None of us like to spend our day around a table, arguing over decisions that aren't really even options. They like to plan the fun out of everything, while we like to get in and out and go home, without having to drag our people to graves in the process." He sighed and closed his eyes. He, like me, was stuck in a memory of burying those we love. After we had come home, the Sluagh had carried the bodies back of those who had died at the hands of mortals, and the Aos Si cleaned and wrapped each one before taking them back to their families for burial. "The others like to play the game of pretending we're not going to do what must be done and forget about those who must carry out those orders. I'm tired of killing everyone in my way, just for another day in Elphame. It's not worth it anymore. If we can't make the situation better, what the hell are we even doing? If we can't end the suffering, the solution can't be to add even more suffering."

"Aren't you a practical bunch?" I stared at the wall, then back to Finn. "I agree with you. Going to bed every night with someone else's blood under my nails isn't worth the extra day I'm given."

"We have a different way if you're willing to try?"

I nodded. "This is going to hurt."

"Everything hurts in Elphame, so what does it matter if we feel the pain today or tomorrow?" he replied.

"What the hell are you planning?" I asked, and he grabbed me.

We landed in the field in front of the Gate. It shimmered as always but was tainted in red streaks. It reminded me of blood in the water...so much death. I could feel it grip the bottoms of my boots as I walked, like sticky paper. Being this close to the Gate again made my stomach twist. I breathed out my anxiety and focused on why we were there this time, not what brought me to the Gate the last time. The Aos Si and Sluagh all stood in a circle around the border into the mortal world. My eyes found Milo immediately, and I smiled. I had wondered where he'd taken off to, since he was usually close by, and I hadn't seen him yet today. It appeared a roast sandwich could bribe him into doing a great many things.

I followed Milo's gaze to the tree line. Between the Court of Less and Blood and Bones, dozens of dragons were stationed. "Dragon scouts, against who? Are we invading Whitwick?"

"Not today, little Crow." Aeden stepped forward, and I smiled to see him again. "We have about twenty minutes before anyone knows what we're doing."

"Rest assured, Solas already knows I'm here. He knew something was up the moment he saw Finn at Blood and Bones. The very wind has eyes and ears for his throne. If he knows, Zephyr will soon find out," I answered. "What's the plan?"

"Jayde has been doing research to help you in return for your helping us." He answered the question on the tip of my tongue, why he was here. His partner was the reason. It didn't surprise me.

"Aeden, do you think Jayde would mind if I came over to talk?" I asked. "After we do whatever the hell you've got planned for the day? If I live through it, that is."

"He's been waiting for you. He figured, one day, you'd want your truth back," Aeden answered. Jayde could feel emotions and see what happened to cause them. He could read impressions and tell you the truth behind the curtains. It was both his strength and a curse he carried with him. Such was the way in Elphame. There is a flip side to every magick and ability...the good and the bad.

"Thank you. Tell Jayde I'll come in the next few days, *if* I am still alive."

Finn passed me a book from Aeden's hand. "You once said that you'd give anything for this to end. I told you I'd come to you if I ever found a way to end this, the Gate. That day is today."

I opened the book and glanced at Aeden. "How did you get this out of Faolan's library? I can smell Christmas on these pages."

"Faolan gave it to Nix, who gave it to Finn, who gave it to me," Aeden answered. "We didn't steal it, if that's what you're thinking. When Nix was trading apple jam with Oisin, Oisin had asked how you were doing. Nix mentioned the Gate would forever cause you pain, but he didn't know how to help you. Faolan showed up with that book. It's the entire history of the Gate and the rift."

Finn smiled, but I could see nervousness behind his grin. "He told Nix to tell you not to rip this one apart for your answers. He wants it back in one piece. But here's your chance, Perdi, to close it for good — to close the actual rift between our worlds, not just the Gate. The energy that keeps this rift open between worlds, close it, and there will never be a place to create a Gate again. There will never be a path between worlds. You could end it all. You could wake up tomorrow, and this could all be over. You'd be stuck here for the rest of time, but that cursed thing will never hurt anyone again. No one will ever die for it again."

My mouth dropped open, and I almost laughed. "That's your plan? To blow me up? I can't hold that much power. Hell, to close the Gate the first time killed me, and that's a smaller task than what you're proposing. The amount it would take to close off the rift holding the door between realms open would boil my blood and fry my brain. And if I survived — which is a really big *if* — I'd cook off my soul. I don't know if you've noticed, but my soul is already a bloody mess and barely holding on. I can't do this, Finn. I'm not strong enough."

"You can, and you are," Finn answered. "If you were inside the Gate, and we all went in there with you, you could spread it around. We can hold as much power as you can. It could be done if we shared the burden, all of us together. The Sluagh will keep us safe. And, if necessary, they'll eat whatever energy we can't take."

"The only burden we'd be sharing is death," I replied. "We'd all probably die in there — all of us together, dead, like one big, happy family."

Finn nodded. "That is probably true."

"You're willing to die to close the rift, to end the Gate for good?" I asked.

"Yes, I am. It'll save your people and mine," Finn replied. "Perdi, this will save you from a lifetime of suffering for this Gate. It will save the rest of us from having to kill the mortal world, because that's what it'll eventually take to keep them from poking their fool heads in here."

I shook my head. "I'm not willing to die for this."

"Then you'll have to work harder to live," he replied.

"This is a bad idea," I muttered.

"You passed on my first suggestion. I was ready to kill everyone at Blood and Bones, but you said no. So here we are. Option two." Finn clapped my shoulder. "I'm fine if we die, Perdi. Because if we don't, Solas will make us all wish for it, for risking your life, while Zephyr eats the souls of those who got away."

I felt a small ping in the pit of my stomach. "Zephyr knows I'm not at Blood and Bones. He's on his way, and he's not happy."

"We haven't much time, then." Finn held out his hand to me. "But before we do this, you need to know, we'll never escape the notice of the Gods. Once, maybe…but never twice. Are you willing to gamble, to end this once and for all? Because if you're willing for the very Sidhe to collect our debt, so am I."

"Today looks like a good day to die," I replied. "It'll take all our blood to do this, and it's going to hurt like hell. When we get in there, fill the space with energy, as much as you can, without draining yourselves. Without the energy, we'll suffocate before we can finish this fool's errand." I looked back toward Blood and

Bones and knew Zephyr and Solas were coming. I grinned as I heard Zephyr's voice on the wind, *foolish little Crow*, followed by Solas' voice, telling me to burn it all to the ground. "Let's go."

"Let's see how closely the Gods are actually watching us, shall we?" Finn said to the others, who smiled in return.

Collectively, we all stepped into the Gate, and my stomach flopped in worry, memory and the initial pangs of regret. If I lived, the payment would probably kill me anyway. If I died, it didn't matter. I wouldn't care about the fallout. The dead don't care about a damn thing. *Lucky bastards*. I pulled the energy tightly around us. I willed the wall between worlds to hold us in and Elphame out. Milo and his people stood around the Gate in Elphame. The Aos Si stood around me in the Gate. All of them rubbed the energy from their arms, not used to standing inside the Gate, only passing through. I wanted to tell them not to bother. It was only going to get worse. But after a few passing glances, they all seemed to realize that things were about to get horrible for us all.

"Nothing is free," I called out to them. "You're going to wish you stayed home today."

I pulled the blade from Finn's thigh holster and sliced my hand. I dragged the knife across Finn's hand, who winced at the pain, which made me smile. The others mirrored Finn and me. In a circle, each sliced their hands. The power filled the small space, and I staggered. The two worlds the rift stood between swirled around us, drinking in the power that flowed from our veins. Each beat of our hearts charged the air like static. The very wind filled with enough energy to feel like glass shards. I closed my eyes and opened my arms, drawing in what I could, to the brink of pain. The first drip of blood fell from my nose — hot, wet and sticky — and I knew I'd bleed a hell of a lot more before this was over.

"Drink it down, boys. The ride has only just begun," I yelled over the wind that had pulled my hair from my braid and twisted it around like a forest fire.

The inside of the Gate looked like a tornado had formed and twisted each of us in a different direction. Finn and Aeden grabbed my hands to keep me from being blown around. All Aos Si had long hair, and it whipped around us, landing like tiny lashes on our arms. Beyond the wind, as the power grew, I could hear the song that created the Gate, a low rumble that shook the ground. With my eyes closed, I could see the original Gate. Two trees, one in Elphame and one in Whitwick, with a small metal Gate in between. Years of bloody war had tarnished the metal and rusted it into ruin. What had once meant the joining of worlds was warped into the brutal fates of thousands. In the distance, I could see Solene inspect each mortal dragged through the Gate. I watched each Crow tearfully pass, never to be seen again. I watched Fae crawl through — some happy, some filled with rage for the task at hand — and countless witches in between, who tried, only to fail at closing the Gate.

I looked beyond where the Gate once stood, into the magick that held it in place. Rather than focus on the passage between worlds, I followed the magick sustaining the pathway. I could almost see the rift, like a wound in the air. As energy poured into the Gate, energy also poured out. I followed the song, the hum that had always been there, under all the noise of magick and power. I dropped to my knees and pushed my bloody hands into the earth and willed life where there had only been death. The grass was coated in drops of our blood, saturating the dry land to life.

The Gate between worlds was truly gone. I knew, with enough power, I could create it anew. I could regrow the grass, sprout the trees and wire a new Gate between Elphame and Whitwick. And as I breathed in the energy that rolled around me and watched souls cross to never be seen again, I knew the Gate was never meant to be there. The rift between worlds shouldn't be there. We would always war over it, perverse the power drawn from it into grotesque fates. There would never be peace because none of us were peaceful creatures. The Gate was war and death, and we all lived and breathed for its control.

I was tempted by faint promises of a time long gone. If I found another Finis, I could tear the rift open and nothing could stand in our way. Just one more Crow, and maybe they would be the one we're looking for. Just one more soul, and perhaps this could end. The only promise that had come true was that mortals died countless deaths as though they had never existed. And they would continue to perish at the hands of Elphame until the world between here and there was dead and gone. I shook the memories that hung inside the rift until only the truth remained. The rift had to close, or we'd never know safety or peace. No one would know freedom again. Whatever the cost would be, I was willing to pay it.

"It's time," I yelled and moved to the middle of our circle. I drank down the power freely given by the men around me and whispered the fate of us all into the rift between worlds.

With knot one, the spell has begun.
With knot two, my heart is true.
With knot three, so mote it be.
With knot four, the rift is no more.
With knot five, all our people shall thrive.
With knot six, the rift will never fix.
With knot seven, the Gate never again be risen.
With knot eight, this spell is our fate.
With a knot of nine, the cost is mine.
So mote it be.

My scream was echoed by the Aos So, who suffered with me, as the power burst out of them and was funneled through me. Our magick filled the mist of the Gate and patched every hole and tear. The rift between worlds began to mend like wounded tissue healed over time. But for the briefest of moments, we were not alone in the Gate. Whoever stood on the other side saw us as I had seen them — on the other side, a whole different realm. Both Finn and I looked at each other. He had seen it too.

"Finvarra..." A woman's voice whispered through the magick and wind. "Perdita..."

Both Finn and I cringed at the calling of our names. His eyes were as wide as mine were. Her voice was familiar, and I glared into the rift. She *was* the Gate, the hate I had felt, the warnings given, the threats made. Before she, on the other side of the rift, could look farther, I slammed the door shut between us. Once the rip between worlds was fully mended, the power had nowhere left to go. It blew outward, ripping down the shimmering wall and blasted us all through the air. I landed in a crunch and stared up at the sky as I relearned how to breathe.

"Foolish little Crow." Zephyr leaned over me and shook his head. "Hold on, Perdi. Your ride has only just begun."

I couldn't breathe. I couldn't focus. I could only lay there and pay for magick that was far greater than I was. It burst within, and I screamed wordlessly. Milo curled around me but couldn't eat my payment. His thunder of dragons sat on his back. Small vibrations from the dragons rolled through Milo and into my body, calming my muscles enough for me to breathe again.

"I wondered why the dragons have been following you," Zephyr said, smiling. "They come to most Finis fledglings, but it has been many moons since they'd chosen a Soul-Eater with a worthy enough soul to follow. And like the Sluagh, dragons can't eat your pain, but they can keep it from killing you."

"Still hurts," I groaned. I could feel the energy moving between me, Milo and a handful of dragons. It was enough to keep my head above water but not enough to think I could do it again.

"Be thankful you're still alive to feel the pain," Zephyr replied.

Finn crawled to my side, and when his hand linked with mine, the pain was shared, and my blood calmed its threat of boiling me alive. The pain in my head eased enough for me to think.

"The cost is *ours*," Finn muttered as he gritted his teeth in pain. I could hear dozens of voices, each sharing the cost of magick. "Oh, my God, it hurts to breathe."

"Everyone...make it?" I grunted out the words around waves of pain.

"If this doesn't kill us, yes," Aeden groaned from a few feet away.

"It's not over," I whispered, and my teeth started to mash against each other. "Only...beginning."

"I don't like pain," Finn moaned.

"Did you see, Finn?" I asked. "Did you hear your name, too?"

"Yes."

"Where... Who?" I asked.

"I don't know, but I doubt we'll remain ignorant for long. We're not that lucky to escape payment twice." He curled into a ball beside me and pressed his forehead into the crook of his arm. I knew exactly what he was feeling—I felt it myself—like his head was about to explode from the pressure. "This feels like every war I've ever fought, at once. Everything hurts. Sweet mercy, is this what your payment is?"

"Usually worse," I groaned. "Sharing makes it easier. Stop fighting it, or it'll be much worse and last even longer."

"This is not my idea of easy," Aeden groaned from beyond Finn. "Next time you need help, Finn, leave me the hell out of it. Goddess, take me now. Even my nails hurt."

Zephyr sat beside me and smiled. "I thought of what I would do to you all as punishment for your stupidity, but I think this is payment enough."

"I'd rather you break my legs." Finn twisted beside me. "It burns so bad. I actually smell burned hair."

"You're probably having a stroke," Aeden called out.

Zephyr leaned closer to Finn. "Broken legs can be done, little soldier. The next time you lie with Perdi, Solas will break them both. Had it not been for Carver pleading your case, he'd have hunted you down." Zephyr smiled as he said the words, but he wasn't happy. "If you touch my blooded sister like that again, clothed or unclothed, I'll fucking kill you, Finn. I do not like that you smell of Crow feathers. Let this be your last warning. There will *not* be another. I promise you that."

"If I live another day, I look forward to the hunt," Finn replied, then passed out from the pain.

"Everyone has a kink." I tried for a smile but knew it would look like gritting my teeth through the pain. "Finn saved my life. Don't kill him for it."

Zephyr grinned. "I know. Threatening him is the only thing that keeps him on his toes. It lets him know I'm always watching."

"Bully," I muttered and finally cried out from the pain.

Milo moved away from Zephyr to curl onto the ground and pull me into his chest. The next wave of payment washed over me, and I shook. "Solas is coming. He has to calm down most of Elphame, who want to come to see what the little Crow has done now."

I nodded and screamed, tucked into a ball, staring through blurred vision at what was once the shimmering wall of the Gate. It was gone, leaving behind grass and one tree filled with cherry blossoms. Gone was any chance of returning. Gone was my childhood. I said goodbye to that chapter in my life by ensuring no other child would be tainted by the Gate. The last feeling I had before the world tilted and dragged me with it was of Solas picking me up and tucking me inside his darkness. Nothing hurt anymore. His cool touch put out the flames. The little bits of pain flowed between us. He took as he always did. He ate what I couldn't handle. He suffered for me, as I knew he would. It didn't matter how many nightmares the witches had forced down my throat. It would never change who I knew he was. He was the man who would come for me in my darkest moments, and he'd kill anyone who stood in his way. As unsettling as it was to know he'd kill his way through any realm to reach me, it calmed my fears in the only way he could.

"Perdi, you've come closer to death since becoming a Crow than I have in all my years in Elphame," Solas whispered.

"It's over," I whispered back. "Worth it."

"Home?" he asked, lifting his eyebrows in question.

"Our home," I replied. "Let's go home."

"*Sleep*. I'll be here. I won't leave you. I promise." He breezed across his territory, passing hundreds of Fae who had come when they felt the Gate truly and utterly gone.

Chapter Fifteen

A wedding in Elphame was not the same as in Whitwick Gates, and I was thankful for that. There wasn't an official ceremony, not like what I was used to. I stood in the middle of the field, alone with Solas, far from the eyes and ears of Fae. He wore color for once, dark blue. It was a start. I wore black because some things never change. My red hair whipped around him in the wind as we stood holding hands. It was bittersweet to stand with him in a place I was raised to hate, after closing myself off from a world I loved less and less with each day that passed. My heart was both filled and empty. What I wouldn't have given to have my father at my side. Even though his life had been stolen from him, I knew he'd given it for me. There was never a day in my life when I didn't know he had given everything for me to survive. Before he'd died, he got to see his dreams come to fruition. He explored the untouchable lands of Elphame and saw his daughter safely into the arms of a man who would keep the monsters at bay. I let go of the rest and held on to the parts I knew had made his final moments mean something more than a pointless death.

"I oath myself to you," Solas said. "For all I am, I am nothing without you."

His words carved over my soul like a lover's touch. "I oath myself to you. For all I am, I've become with you."

"And so shall we make this oath," he replied, slicing open his hand.

"And so shall the oath be written in our blood," I answered, dragging a knife over my hand and pressing it into his.

The moment our blood mixed, my body burst into darkness. I smelled the night like I held all of it in the palm of my hand. Where our hands touched, my skin slowly covered in the night sky. His very darkness now rolled inside me, and it felt like coming home. He wrapped his arms around me and told me to hold on. Before I asked, the night poured from our skin and lifted us off the ground. He carried me back to the manor on wind I could now feel in my very soul.

"Hold on." I winked.

He gripped the headboard. "What are you...?"

His words trailed off as I kissed his lips and unleashed my Malice. She slinked into his soul, not starved, but in joining. His muscles stood firm under his flesh as he fought not to let go of the bed. He jerked at first and finally relaxed once he knew my Malice had come in peace and not her usual war. He released his darkness, and they swam together. We both shuddered when our souls touched, and they twisted themselves around each other. It felt like we had spent an eternity in those moments as our oaths slid between us, covering our souls, becoming one. I understood why oathed mates were hell on wheels. The thought of someone stepping between Solas and me made me think some of the darkest thoughts.

Solas pulled me into a kiss. "Like you, I'd do wicked things to protect you."

"You say the sweetest things to me," I replied. "I love you. I always have and always will."

When I climbed into the shower, he followed, and we spent an hour trying to prepare for our oathing party. But the idea of leaving the comfort of our shared darkness was less appealing with each move toward the door. The banquet, we missed, both unwilling to leave the bedroom or the peace we found in each other's arms. We filled the night with love and healing...and comfort. The rest could always come tomorrow. The Court didn't stop, not even for this, but it could wait. Right now, home was where we both needed to be. For me, it was in Elphame, with Solas, with my family and friends, both new and old, and with a Gate that would never return. I hadn't mourned the loss of my way back to the mortal world. There was no room in that realm for little Crows or Soul-Eaters.

We left pieces of ourselves from one end of Elphame to the other. In the mortal realm, we left those pieces for the birds when we closed the rift between worlds. The cost of it all, I didn't pay alone. But the payment made to get home to Solas, to bring our people home, was a cost none of us wanted to pay. Finn became a monster and still struggled to look himself in the eyes. And I became everything I was meant to be. And now the world knew there were two of us. Two Soul-Eaters in a world that hadn't even wanted one. But now, there was nowhere left for my enemies to hide. That should have made it easier to sleep at night. It didn't. I had taken away their hiding spot, cornering them like animals. As I could attest to, a cornered animal always bites. This Crow certainly did—and I'd do it again.

Want to see more from this author? Here's a taster for you to enjoy!

A Cursed Crow: The Last Crow
Lanne Garrett

Excerpt

Time, like so much else in Elphame, moved differently for peace than it did for war. The moments you wanted to hold on to for the longest sped by as if they hadn't happened at all. I had come to Elphame a Crow, fated to die on Fae soil, through a Gate that was no longer. It felt like I had lived several lifetimes within a short period, and each day had tested me and prepared me for what was coming next. Some of my memories were brief and fading, while others take up more room in my soul than needed. But that was the fate of us all, to earn moments worth remembering, because nothing is free in Elphame, especially the good parts.

As I contemplated where I had ended up, where I had fought to get to, I sat in the trees with a picnic packed for me by Solas. I could already smell the mashed potatoes and apple turnovers...the two things that reminded me of home, comfort and people I loved dearly. Although I complained about the potatoes more often than not, the day I stopped seeing them would break my heart. It was the small things that could make or break my day. I dug through my lunch bag, decorated with a small black crow, and traded Finn my sugary treats for his apple. With frosted grapes from the Winter Court in my hand, I sank into the sun's heat with a friend who'd torn his soul apart to get me back to Elphame, because that's what family did for each other. They burned off parts of themselves for you to survive.

Finn's dark head rested on a rock, two feet to my right, under the trees. He was dressed head to toe in black leathers and always looked ready to fight a war, should the opportunity arise. He was telling me of my secret birthday party I wasn't to know about, on pain of death at Nix's hands. In a few months, I'd celebrate another year I've lived through, a milestone in a place like this. I'd spent my first birthday in this place in the Golden Courts, watching people die. The second one, I'd barely made it to in one piece. I had torn myself apart, heart and soul, for another year of Elphame. And another long year is what I'd got. Pinnacle moments between each of those long years had risen like waves and crashed down like thunder, threatening to drag away everything good and everyone I loved. I held on for dear life during each storm, even though my arms got tired and I almost lost my grip a few times. It wasn't lost on me why Fae stopped counting their years. Reflecting back over a year of hell didn't sound like the best way to start a new one.

I didn't go far from the manor anymore without someone with me — someone who would die in my place, slowly enough for me to escape. The Dark Courts weren't a prison, as it had been before, but I was cautious of the limits of my safety. I didn't test them as I once had. Now, it was just simply smart not to be alone. It wasn't often I was seen without the Aos Si or the shadows. It wasn't worth the argument to leave them behind. We were family, and you didn't leave your family to face the world alone. After being to hell and back on more than one occasion, I had agreed to one guard when I left the yard. I didn't mind it now that I didn't feel caged. With the Aos Si, it felt like I was spending my time with a friend, and it gave Solas and Zephyr the freedom to do their duties and not need to stop and check in on me. Their trust in my complete safety would never come, but their belief that others would die for me was enough to not spend their days looking over their shoulder for me.

On the back hills of Autumn Court, which had been swallowed by the Court of Less, Finn and I relaxed after hours with Jayde. Jayde, a man of many talents, could help you unpack your emotional baggage in a way no one else could. He could pull the nightmares from my mind and dissect them with love and compassion, allowing me to let them go. And for Finn and me, we had more than enough damage between us both to keep Jayde busy until the end of his days. We had killed an island-full of people, which was the start of our shared wound. Then we'd eaten an entire village of people together. That tends to leave bruises on souls and gouged at dreams. The shame would always remain, but it had lessened enough over time that I could see my reflection in the mirror and not cringe. I could look myself in the eyes and forgive myself—not for every death, but it was a start.

The sessions with Jayde were healing, but it was the screams, giggling and interruptions from children that made my time spent with him mean something more. Seeing what Jayde and Aeden were building in a world with little room for greatness gave me a sense of peace. What they were doing with their home, opening it to the children of Elphame, is what truly scabbed the wounds and gave me hope that my life could mean something more one day. Their home was everything Aeden had dreamed of and more. A walk down any hallway would show you just that. Walls were decorated with painted pictures, cutouts of hands and feet, flowers and monsters, and drawings of happy memories. Rooms weren't prepared for banquets. They were decorated for tea parties. Furniture wasn't arranged for the kings and queens of Elphame. Instead, the rooms held blanket forts and castles for tiny princes and princesses. Every space was filled with life and love, promises of futures and new beginnings. Seeing that made my wounds seem smaller in some way — that even in the worst of times, when everything you loved had been taken from you, you could find it again and rebuild.

The moment I stepped onto the path to their house, I smiled right down to my soul. This was a home in every sense of the word for all who needed one, from the off-duty Aos Si doing laundry and carting children under their arms like sacks of flour, to the guards cooking and laughing together at puppet shows and pictures painted of them and those from various courts who volunteered. This was a new beginning for those who needed one, not only for the children. It was fitting that I had found my way to their door to rebuild myself, as so many others had before me. Within those walls, my secrets stayed, my fears were put to rest and I was forgiven for deeds I'd sooner not do again.

For weeks after I emerged from my father's home, I had visited the families of those who had come into Whitwick to find me, only to die a horrible death. Each family I grieved with all over again. And as painful as it was, it helped me let go a little bit more each time I faced what had happened to us all. Carver and Finn came with me, and it had allowed them the same release. Nightmares shouldn't be faced alone. Today, I unpacked a little more baggage with Jayde and bandaged old wounds. With Finn, we'd let the lingering pain go as we ate our picnic and waited on Solas and Zephyr to join us. This evening, we were removing my morbid garden from behind the manor, the last dark memory to let go of. Many laughs had come from the garden, but it tethered us to moments we didn't want each time we stood on my balcony. Orrian had already picked through it and carried away the plants she wanted to line her border with. The rest would be burned, along with the memories attached to them. Nix would bring the marshmallows, and the Winter Court would come with frost wine. This wasn't just about healing myself. This was about us all learning to leave the past where it belonged...behind us.

"Why do you always look like you're about to go to war, Finn?" I asked, pulling my hair onto my shoulders so the sun that broke through from the trees wouldn't burn me. From the grounds of Autumn Court, the sun always left a mark on my pale, freckled skin. I was made for darkness, from my soul to my flesh. "I've never seen you not strapped to the teeth with weapons. None of you are ever casually dressed. Is it an Aos Si rule?"

"Not a rule, but a lesson learned by us all. To stand this close to the throne, one learns to either be ready to fight or we die pretty damn fast," Finn answered and breathed in the air between us. "And why are you *not* prepared for war? I can smell only one knife. Have you learned nothing from your broken wings? You don't just stand close to the throne, Perdi. You *are* the throne.

After what you've been through, I'd think you'd be tired of running for your life."

I knew he'd smell the cleaner I had used on my blade. Even I could smell it. But it was still unsettling how accurate his sense of smell was. "Some of us don't want war."

"I didn't say I wanted a war, but I do want to live another day bad enough to be prepared to fight for it. The sooner you figure that out, the sooner you stop leaving chunks of yourself all over the damn place. Cleaning up crow feathers isn't a walk in the park for any of us." He grinned. Finn had the knack of jamming the truth down my throat and making me laugh as if I hadn't just choked on what he had said. "If you had to choose between fighting Aos Si or the Royal Guard, which one would you choose?"

I laughed. It reminded me of the nights I had spent with the Aos Si trainees, trying to find Solas and Zephyr. They bridged the gap between home and hell with stories and laughter as we sat on an island and hunted a population of Fae who had been hidden from the rest of the world for so long that when we were done, they were entirely forgotten by everyone but us. I breathed in my regret and let it flow back out into the world that had helped create it. We all felt the cost of that rescue, but today it didn't sting as much as it had a few months before.

"Royal Guard, hands down. I train with you all. The Aos Si are brutal. I don't have a hope in hell of winning," I answered. "Every chance you guys get, you kick my butt."

"But there's way more of the Royal Guard that you'd have to beat than Aos Si," he countered.

"The numbers game isn't what I'd worry about. It's the strength of those I'd have to fight. Each Aos Si is an army on their own. It's like having to fight a few dozen at once, who are deadlier, faster, stronger and much more conniving than the Royal Guard will ever be. Plus, if I waged war against the Royal Guard, you'd all come to help me. If I fought you guys, who the hell would be brave enough to show up? Zephyr wouldn't. He'd want me to learn some lesson by taking you all on at once. Solas might, though. I think I'd win if he helped," I answered and tilted my head in wonder. "Finn, why don't the Aos Si guard thrones or courts? You can leave the Aos Si and become a Royal Guard, but you don't do both. Aside from Zephyr, almost none of you are around unless he's nearby. The trainees are around, but only if I'm there."

"The Aos Si have never guarded a royal in Elphame, not since the days of the original court in Blood and Bones. We're war and peace and justice, and we can't be that if we've picked a side from the start. Although we follow Zephyr, who chooses to follow Solas, we'd never fight for him if Solas waged war for territory or power. We don't come for every battle. Most aren't worth our time or energy, and we'd never come for grabs of power. We're only there when it's worth our notice or intervention."

"I haven't been here long enough to know, but have you ever stood for a different court?"

"We don't even stand for *this* court, Perdi. We stand with people, regardless of their crown. Lucky for you, the Dark Court doesn't wage frivolous wars, and never has Solas attacked an encampment of innocents. But, to answer your question, it isn't often we've found ourselves on the other side of the river, in Seelie territory, given their thirst for power and all-encompassing dominance. But we've stood for other courts and intervened on their behalf when the innocent were at risk. We've been sent to help move people from the front lines before we've gone to war against their kings." His answer made more sense than it would have a couple of years before when my hands were clean of blood. "If we did guard, as you've asked, you wouldn't see us. Solas doesn't put his strongest around his throne. He puts them around his people. Have you ever heard him command his army to protect his crown? It's always his people he protects first—his family, innocents caught between his decisions. Hell, when he was taken by the Satyr, he had the chance for freedom, and he chose to stay to save his people. That's one of the reasons I'd stand at his side. He has honor," Finn replied, and we both shuddered as those memories of the island came and went. Neither of us was fully healed from the decisions we had to make and the ones forced upon us. "In any other court, we go straight for the throne. Their kings protect themselves over their own people. The strongest of their army can be found guarding the king. It's pitiful but predictable. And once their throne falls, the rest is just cleanup. Here, in the Dark Courts, I'd never make it to your front door, with or without the Aos Si guarding. I'd die in the field, where those more powerful would be stationed. And if I managed to get past them, I have to fight off the Sluagh and whatever the hell lives in these forests. Solas' throne isn't worth the trouble."

"Why are you with me if you never guard a royal?" I asked.

"I'm not here to guard you, but I'd protect you if needed, just like you would help me if I needed it. I'm here as your friend, and no one gets to choose who my friends are, regardless of which court they're from or how close to the throne they sit. When we're like this, you're just Perdi, and I'm just Finn. Neither of us must be what the fates forced us to become. We don't have to hide who we are from each other." His expression changed just enough for me to notice that his mind was in a dark place. "When I'm with you, I feel at peace with my decision to get back here. When I'm able to be here like this, I have no regrets about the life I've chosen to have, not even the broken parts and pieces. I don't have to be who I was born to be. I can just be myself." He rolled onto his back and tossed a cherry into his mouth, moving a knotted stem to his lips. He wiggled his eyebrows.

I yanked the stem from his teeth. "Keep it up, and you will have a very short life."

"There's no better reason to die than for love," he answered.

"You flirting with me is not a reason to die."

"Your ego is almost as big as Nix's." He laughed until I watched him wipe the tears from his eyes. "I'm not flirting with you, Perdi. I love you, but not as a lover would. I love you as you would a friend you've had for an entire lifetime. I do these tricks because I know Zephyr is always watching us, and it drives him up the wall. He's so bloody protective over you. It's entertaining. He's petty about it, and I always look forward to his chats after we part."

"Do you enjoy his beatings that much?" I laughed.

"There's a kink for everyone. Maybe I like the pain." He laughed back.

I inched myself to the ground beside him and stared up at the sky, little bits of light falling down through the leaves. "I don't think you like the pain any more than I do."

"But we were made to suffer — and suffer we shall," he replied. He tossed a handful of cherries into the trees behind us and grinned ear to ear when the dragons scurried out to fetch them. It was the smallest things that brought him the most joy. Finn loved that the dragons were back to roaming Elphame, and he could be found daily, feeding them in the backyard. He said it signified the return of peace when the smaller creatures were willing to come out of hiding. Seeing any amount of happiness, for any reason, made me feel like the journey, however hard it had been, was worth it. "If you had to fight Solas or me, who would you pick?"

"What is with you guys and your '*would you rather*' questions?" I asked.

"I'm curious who you would pick and how you would win. It tells me if you're brave or stupid and how at risk I am for being this close to you. The throne isn't the only danger, Perdi. *You* are. And your answers tell us what areas you still need training in and what lessons Zephyr is yet to teach you."

"Makes sense. For the record, though, I'm probably more stupid than brave...or a combination of both," I answered. "Solas... I'd pick him to fight."

"You don't think he'd beat the tar out of you?"

"Oh, he'd win a thousand times over. But with Solas, I know who and what I'm fighting. I know how he fights and what he uses to fight with. I know he'd win in a hand-to-hand fight, but he'd hesitate to kill me. With you, I simply don't know."

"You know me, Perdi."

I rolled to face him. "No, I don't think I do. I know what you show me but nothing more. I have your pearl, but when I touch it, I feel nothing beyond what I already know. I don't see your past, your memories or your truths. I see bits and pieces, but it's like trying to find a diamond in the mud. When the light hits it just right, I see a faint twinkle, but not enough to snatch it.

Sometimes, when you're dreaming and it's as horrible as my own, I can feel you and hear you scream, but I don't know what you're dreaming of. That's as close to your truth as I get without you telling it to me."

"Yet, you trust me. I feel that. I also feel your love."

I breathed him in. "Yes, I do. You feel like home."

"Feel, not smell? You usually tell people they remind you of a smell from home or a memory of something you treasure."

I shook my head. "You smell of here, familiar scents that remind me of places I like to visit and moments I don't want to forget. But you *feel* like here, *all* of here. Every scent you have is of every place in Elphame. I don't know what is you and what is merely where you've been. It's odd. Everyone else smells of their court, but you smell of everywhere. And when I'm around you, I always feel like I'm right here, in the Dark Courts. It doesn't really matter where I am. If you're there, it feels like that exact spot could be home. And for everything I feel when I'm with you, I know so little about you. Your pearl isn't empty, but I can't understand what it tells me. The odd time I've felt your magick, I've always backed up rather than tried to understand it. My Malice isn't sure of what she's feeling, and it makes her nervous not to know."

"I didn't know you couldn't read my pearl."

I shrugged. "I'm not as talented as Zephyr."

"You could just simply ask, like Zephyr did," he replied. "I think you depend on those pearls a little more than you do a polite conversation."

"Something's wrong," I whispered as I watched the dragons flare in bright colors in a warning.

The moment I heard Zephyr's name, I could feel him. I scanned the field in front of the tree line and jerked at a boom that blasted across Elphame and rolled across the grass until it slapped my cheek, hard and wet. Both Finn and I jumped while the ground still rumbled from the noise. The dragons surrounding us scattered. Leaves and flower petals swirled in the wind, landing at our feet. It reminded me of thunder and lightning in Whitwick and how it shook you to your core when it hit too close to your house. Across the field, both Solas and Zephyr were coming in a swirl of night and shadows. Their movement dredged up memories of how the fog used to move through Whitwick, and it took everything in my soul not to step back. But I'd be lying if I didn't say I wanted to hide from what I saw.

"Perdi." Finn grabbed my hand. His grip was tight, as if he were tethering me to the ground.

"Whatever it is, I can feel it, too." I held his hand as if it were a life raft. "Don't let go, please. Whatever is coming, I can feel it."

"Not what…who. And they're already here," Finn replied.

"Who is already here?"

"The Sidhe," he answered. A shiver ran down his body and spasmed around my hand. "Fate has finally come to collect her payment for what we've done."

"*The cost of winning will attract the notice of the Gods and Goddesses. A great payment will be made to end the war*," I echoed Lily's words, said as a warning I hadn't listened to. We would pay for how we'd survived our Taking. Finn had said similar when we were in Whitwick, just before we'd unleashed our inner monsters to get home.

"I'd rather face the Gods than what's coming," Finn replied.

Solas and Zephyr reached us and wrapped us within their panic and shadows. Fear and uncertainty were not common emotions to be found in both of them at once. I was smothered between their dread and darkness, as if the night were on fire and pressed down from the clouds. The very air was hot, clammy and heavy as it filled my lungs. A few more gasps reminded me of fighting against a current, trying not to drown.

"I can't breathe," I whispered. "Calm down before I get sick."

"We have no time," Solas started.

"No time for what?" I frowned. "What has happened?"

"The Sidhe has opened. I can feel them." Finn's word carried a weight to them, lost on me but understood by the others.

"The Sidhe hasn't opened since Elphame was born," Solas countered.

"Yet, here they are," Finn replied.

"This is going to hurt, little Crow." Zephyr grabbed my shoulders and turned me to face him. His energy rolled through me and locked my pearls into a cage in my soul. I felt the staggering separation from them. It was like a quick cut, but deep enough for me to want to pull away and protect myself.

"What are you doing?" I asked.

"The Sidhe come for two reasons, war and punishment. We're still standing, so one of us is about to take the brunt of their visit," Zephyr answered. "After thousands of years, we've finally done something so great, they've noticed."

"Why did you lock away my pearls?" I asked.

"Because if it's you that they are here for, you will need them later to survive whatever they decide will be your punishment. They'll take everything else away from you, but they can't take your pearls. Your souls are your power. Locking them away now will keep a

reserve of magick within them that you can use later."
He squeezed my shoulders once and nodded. I didn't
know if he was trying to convince himself or me that
this would be enough to protect me. "I have locked
away my own pearls, as well. And if it is not us they've
come for, we can't allow them to use our pearls to track
our people through us."

My eyes widened. For Zephyr to lock away his main
power source told me this would do more than simply
hurt. "What do you think they want?"

"Not what…who," Finn answered. "And that
would be all or one of us, I imagine."

"Why?" I asked.

"Really? You wonder why the greatest power in all
of Fae wants to talk to the most powerful of Elphame?"
Finn asked, then shook his head. His expression told
me I had asked a stupid question. "Perdi, the list is a
long one for us all. But off the top of my head, I don't
imagine they're happy that we closed the rift."

"Why would they care?" I asked.

"Because the last time they were here was to open
the bloody thing," Finn replied. "The boom is a new
tear in the fabric between our realms."

"Again, I don't understand why they'd care?" I
replied.

"The Sidhe created Elphame, the rift between our
worlds. Blood and Bones used that rift to open a Gate
into the mortal realm. When you also closed it, you shut
the door to the Sidhe."

Solas stared at me, surprised. "You closed the rift
into the Sidhe? You didn't think to mention that?"

I fought the urge to glare at him, my fear inching its
way into anger. "First, I didn't know it was your
creators who made it or owned it. You'd think someone
would have mentioned *that*? Second, what did you

think I did? The doorway between the mortal realm and us wouldn't close for good unless I closed off the energy that kept it open. Where did you think the Gate went? When the shimmering wall fell, what did you think I did? I told you I closed it all for good."

"This is going to hurt," Solas groaned.

"I'm sorry. I didn't know," I mumbled. "I'm sorry, Solas."

"It's okay, Perdi. We've faced hell before. We can do it again. No matter what they say and do, remember who you are and who we are. We are the Dark Court." Solas pulled me in for a hug. His entire body tensed, and he tilted his head, listening to something I could not hear. "Lily is calling us to Blood and Bones. The Sidhe have come through a new rift over the water."

"What do we do?" I asked.

"Bite your tongue as if every word that comes out of your mouth decides the fate of every soul in Elphame...because it does," Zephyr replied.

"I know how to be quiet," I replied.

"No, little Crow, I don't think that's a skill you've mastered." Solas laughed softly, more mournful than happy. "But today will be a good lesson in never missing the opportunity to keep your words to yourself. Remember... The less you say, the less you must explain. The less you must explain, the less they can punish you for," Solas warned. "No one ever forgets their first time with the Sidhe. Remember that. They will teach you hurt you've never known before. The Sidhe are the worst of us, with more power to back up their threats."

"Bloody hell." I swallowed hard. He had once told me the same thing about my first night as a Crow. I turned to Finn. His eyes were ablaze and filled to the brim with worry. "On a scale of being lashed in the

Golden Court to being drained of my blood and cut off from Elphame, how painful will this be?"

"Remember when you asked me how hard I've been hit, and you offered to show me a new measurement of pain? This will be your new measurement. Trust me when I tell you, the Golden Court is but a small sample of what the Sidhe can and will do," he replied. "But this pain will be felt on your soul. Payment to the Sidhe comes in drops of pearls, not blood. You'll ask for the lash when you feel what they offer."

"Oh my God." The very thought of it made me shiver.

"Foolish little Crow, your God isn't here, either," Finn replied. "Now, let's go see what the rift dragged in."

"This is going to hurt," I whispered.

"Unlike anything you've ever felt," Finn replied.

About the Author

Lanne Garrett writes books. Considering where you're reading this, it makes perfect sense. She lives in Vancouver, here she spends her days getting lost in the beauty of reading and writing and can be found behind a mountain of books on any given Sunday.

Lanne loves to hear from readers. You can find her contact information, website details and author profile page at https://www.finch-books.com

Sign up for our newsletter and find out about all our romance book releases, eBook sales and promotions, sneak peeks and FREE romance books!